So Thankful

TABOO TOMES

ARIA DAZE

Dedicated to Shon The Author. She encouraged me to get a little wild by dipping my toe into the taboo side of things. So you have her to thank, dear reader.

Contents

Content Warnings!

Before you dive in, please check out these handy content warnings. Reading should be enjoyable, and some of the topics covered in this book may not be for you. Your mental health matters.

This book will definitely include the following:

- Penetrative sex

- Oral sex

- Estranged family dynamics

- Neglect of an adult child

- Anxiety

- Post-military service PTSD

- May contain passages of incest, knowingly and unknowingly committed.

- Foul language

This book also features black people who utilize Ebonics in their speech. It's not country, improper, or ghetto, and I would not like to see any emails about it. Please feel free to email me about other things though, such as the hair washing scene. As always, if any of these topics sound unpleasant to you, please do not continue onward, dear reader. I have other things in my catalog that may be a better fit. **This book is not suitable for readers under the age of 18!**

The playlist

Reckless- Arin Ray
Gone- Alex Isley
Sweetest Taboo - Sade
Is It A Crime?- Sade
Get To Know Ya- Maxwell
Love And Happiness - Al Green
Take You There- H.E.R.

Genesis

(THE BEGINNING OF THE END)

Mars- Sometime in the future

Have you ever been in the middle of sudsing up your ass when you were struck with the sudden and uncontrollable urge to fart? No? Liar. Anyway, I ask because that's how it felt when I found out the truth about my now wife. It was a betrayal I never saw coming, and it's one that I've never fully recovered from either. The truth, although unpleasant, reminded me of a natural constant. Life was a series of ups and downs. I almost had the satisfaction of falling in love easy and clean, but then someone just had to go and shit all over it. For a while after everything went down, I lived in constant emotional agony, wondering what I did to deserve such fate. Did I piss off Big Sandals in a past life? I don't know, who's to say. In the end everything did work out, but not without a lot of soul searching. I can't tell you why life chose this path for us, but what I can tell you is where it all began. Four winters ago in Texas.

Mars- January 2025

Men are visual creatures, and most can relate to love at first sight .But not me. Instead I fell in love a second after I heard Cleo address my person for the first time. Her voice was a divine modulation of paced breaths, syrupy giggling, and Southern soothsaying. Something so beautiful that it brought visions of heaven down to the sticky grocery store aisle I stood in on Earth, and when I turned around to see what all the fuss was about, I was pleasantly surprised to see that her face was identically striking. I watched her lips round at the end of her request, while her eyes lifted up with a gentle smile. Whatever she said was probably clever, but I couldn't understand a word she was saying with the chorus of trumpets and harps sounding in my head. However, whatever it was made me less pissy about the 31° high.

I didn't mind the cold, but the one thing I couldn't fucking stand is ice. Ice should be rare in Texas seeing as we're just a sneeze away from the border, but as with lots of rare events these days, it's becoming more and more common. And of course I'm the only one with the tires to handle it, which means I'm perpetually on salt duty. My sisters got on my nerves, but I wouldn't leave them hanging during any severe weather. So I layered up, scraped my windshield clean, and headed off to all the low-key spots to get last minute salt.

That brought me to the Asian Supermarket on Bingum street, three feet in front of the love of my life, who was looking at me like I shit my pants.

"I'm sorry," I snapped after shaking my trance. "What did you say?"

"I said, I'm sorry for bothering you, but can you please hand me that yellow spice pack? I'm too short to reach out without climbing on the shelves. S-santa left behind an elf."

My hand shot up and grabbed the requested item before she could finish speaking. her sentence. Ga Vi Nau Pho Bac. It was staple at a lot of Vietnamese restaurants, and her basket had everything to make the perfect pot of Pho broth, including shanks, oxtail, and plenty of herby aromatics.

"Noodles tonight?" I asked as I placed her spices in the cart.

"Tomorrow," she nodded. "It's last minute because I didn't think it'd get so cold down here."

"Yeah, unfortunately. Texas is a mixed bag," I agreed while eyeing her. "But where are you from?"

I knew it was a personal question immediately after I asked it. Miss spice bag's eyebrows shot up into her hairline, then I heard my dearly departed mother's voice chastising me for being such an inconsiderate creep. She had raised me better than that, as all of her phantom fussing indicated, but this time I couldn't help myself. There was profound need aching in my chest. The need to know everything about the woman in front of me. Including all of her corny jokes, her Pho preferences, and where in the country she potentially saw us living in five to ten years.

"I'm sorr-" I started to apologize.

"I'm from Hot Springs," she interjected.

"Arkansas?"

"The one and only."

"I'm sorry that was a dumb question," I admitted. "I haven't done this in a while."

"Done what?" she tittered with an adorable head tilt.

"Ask a pretty woman out to dinner," I grinned.

I hadn't asked anyone out to dinner in years, actually. Turning twenty eight brought me some much needed clarity about who I was and what I wanted out of life, which didn't necessarily align with the women I generally pursued.

But now seven years had passed and my gut told me she could be different.

Maybe we'd go on a date, hit it off, fall in love, then spend the rest of our days telling each other corny ass jokes. Maybe she could cook the sides while I cooked the meats, and maybe Hot Springs would be better suited for all of that instead of Beaumont. I'd give my last pair of drawls to find out, but first I just needed her to say…"Depends."

"Depends?" I gasped. "On what exactly?"

"Depends on if you're asking me to an actual date, or if this is just a housing application to get out of the cold," she sighed matter of factly.

I tried not to laugh in her face but a snicker did escape me. Nothing about what she said offended me because I knew plenty of niggas who became romantics in cold weather, especially when they thought they had a victim with low-self esteem. However I had never been that type, and I could tell the short, chubby, angel in front of me was anything but easy. And I liked a challenge.

"Damn Mamas, I give off black trash bag energy?" I chuckled while clutching my chest. "Is it the beanie?"

My father was as old as Abraham when he had me, but that was alright because he taught me a few things before departing. Like how not to take myself too seriously. My laughter encouraged her shoulders to soften as our mutual amusement grew. Then she flashed me a smile. A real one that was unrehearsed, imperfect and full of pearly white teeth.

A smile that I wanted to see for the rest of my life.

"It's the nose ring and the corduroys. I assume they're thrifted?" she queried.

"Hey, I like to save the planet. There's nothing wrong with a little recycled living. Plus I thought the glasses would save me."

"Almost," she giggled. "But they somehow make it worse? I don't know, it's giving toxic R&B king. Like you have clarity but you use it for nefarious purposes."

"Sometimes," I admitted accidentally. "However, I assure you, my Mama raised a gentleman."

"Mhm," she hummed, raising her eyebrow with understandable skepticism. "Is that who's asking me out to dinner? The gentleman?"

"Of course," I grinned, knowing that the gentleman had limited appearances. "So is that a-"

Cleo

"Yes."

I said yes without hesitation to a tall, caramel, demon with blackberry eyes. Now four days had passed and I had learned his name was Mars, much like the God of war. Like the aforementioned God, he had an affinity for the color red, previously served in the military, and enjoyed gardening. I had a feeling that wasn't where the similarities ended either. The sparkle in his eye told me that I had plenty more to discover should I want to.

And as much as I swore up and down I didn't have time for a man and his antics, I wanted to discover everything about him.

That meant I needed to consult the board. Sure the board was all the way in Atlanta, but that was what technology was for. We were always just a phone call away, and the phone only ever had to ring once before she picked up.

"Cleo-patraaaaa," Luci sang as she lept from Ermias' lap. "I thought you abandoned me."

"Luci, don't be dramatic," I sighed. "It's been twelve hours since we last texted."

"Same difference," she shrugged. "What's new boo?"

Luci had a very strong sense of intuition, and I could tell it was hard at work by the smug grin plastered on her face. She'd probably been waiting on me to call her about this for days.

"So," I started carefully. "I may have met a man."

"God damn it!" Ermias cursed before passing her a bill off screen. "I gotta stop taking these bets."

"I keep telling you I know what the fuck I'm talking about," she chortled with a snap of her fingers. "Tell me everything about him, Clo."

"Tallish, bald, wears glasses, funny, but not funny weird, funny haha. He's also hella calm and very take-charge, plus he paid for my groceries."

We had a nice conversation, but him covering me was very unexpected and appreciated. Especially since he didn't do that corny ass shit men usually do when they buy food and insist that I save him a plate. Nope, Mars just paid, told me to enjoy my spoils, and wished me a good night.

And to think I was this close to ordering out instead of cooking.

"You met him when you went out to get Pho stuff?" Luci deduced.

"Mhm," I nodded while picking out a few options. "You were right."

She told me to get out of the house and explore my new city. She said, *"You never know who you'll end up meeting."* At first I brushed it off as her not wanting to see me lonely without her, but then I met Mars.

"So the date is tonight?" she followed up.

"Yes, and I have three potential outfits," I confirmed.

I barely had to hold up the hangers before Luci submitted her choice.

"The black jumpsuit with the bell sleeves. Your titties look insane in that hoe and so do your legs."

"Luci, stop commenting on people's titties," Ermias chided from somewhere in the house.

"It's ok, Erm!" I shouted back. "I asked!"

I did a quick fit check by slipping my legs in the suit before adjusting it against my bust. Holy Tit-ca-moly. Luci was right, this jumpsuit did make my titties look insane, and I didn't even have on a bra.

"You might wanna skip the bra and just do a nip cover or something, friend," she said warily. "Them thangs gone be at your neck otherwise."

It was like she could read my mind.

"Lord, ok. I'm thinking silver jewelry, brown makeup, and the-""Chunky suede booties with the burgundy bottom?" Luci finished. "Hard agree."

Nah, she definitely could. Witchy ass. Knowing her, she probably lit an incense, said a prayer, and divined Mars.

"It's so creepy when you do that," I sighed. "Anyway, how's the girlfriend search going?"

We talked until I gathered everything for my outfit and finished my makeup. Apparently the girlfriend search was going horrendously as someone Ermias met had a really weird fetish for big butts and farts. Luci told me as much as she could about that doozy of a kink before Erm distracted her with caramel drop cookies, then I had to go smoke because my nerves were getting the best of me.

Mars and his charismatic smile was on my mind heavy. The warm brown eyeshadow that I had smudged into my crease even reminded me of him. It was damn near the same color as his eyes, and those eyes with that smile were a lot of trouble. When I first moved I swore to myself and my Luci that I would not be giving any more men the time of day, and especially not these Texas niggas. My mama had plenty of horror stories about the dating scene from when she lived her thirty years previous, and so did my dads. I liked to learn from other people's mistakes so I took everything they told me to heart. Yet all present in my heart and head when I saw Mars included butterflies, stars, and an inkling of hope that his personality matched his face.

Reason and warning had mostly abandoned me.

Which is why he was currently knocking on my door while I stood in the mirror, panic-applying a refresh of lipgloss while spraying myself with perfume to mask any lingering aroma of good kush.

Once I finally got it together, I swung open the door with way too much force. It hit the adjacent wall then did a little shake from the impact. I found it wholly unnecessary and embarrassing, but Mars didn't even flinch. He just smiled down at me like he did the first night we met, before extending me a ridiculous bouquet of amaryllis flowers wrapped in a huge violet bow.

"I hope you don't mind. Truthfully, I was rummaging through your photos on IG and I saw that you mentioned amaryllis being one of your favorite flowers," he explained, bringing a palm to the back of his neck.

I slowly eased the flowers from his grasp, mostly so I could savor the subtle honeyed scent before I needed to part with them. Amaryllis were my favorite flowers, I just couldn't get them often because they had a short season. It had been well over two years since I last had the pleasure of them, which meant...

"Are you talking about the picture where I had one in my hair?" I asked, slightly dumbfounded. "That had to be from at least three years ago."

I stood silently, waiting for someone or something to indicate that this was a joke or somehow a misunderstanding. Something to indicate that the man standing in front of me was not as thoughtful and considerate as he appeared to be. However, it never came. Instead Mars took my free hand, placed my palm in his, and brushed my tight knuckles with his thumb.

"Full disclosure, Cleo. I really like you and I'm fully invested in ensuring that this date goes well for both of us," he said.

Then I recognized another thing he had in common with his namesake.

Passion.

I think you're going to ruin my life, I thought to myself as I swallowed my pounding heart.

Sweet Like Candy

Mars

I was going to fuck this up.

I was sure of it.

Cleo hadn't given me any reason to feel that way, yet logic was warring against fear due to how awkward I was after my dating hiatus. Plus a slightly more pressing concern was the fact that Cleo made me nervous. My heart pounded in my ears every time her smooth acrylics brushed against my hand. My stomach was a mess of fluttering and jumping every time I saw that life-altering smile of hers, and my cheekbones burned every time her melodic laughter filled my ears. It took me twenty minutes to realize that burning feeling was actually blushing, and I didn't even know that was a thing I could do. I was fidgeting, I was rambling, and I was trying so hard not to stare at her titties that bounced with her every breath. Everything about tonight reminded me of the boy I was twenty years ago, who couldn't even form a sentence around his crush.

Cleo didn't seem to notice though. She was still smiling, giggling, and blushing over the amaryllis. Completely unaware that I was consumed with anxiety.

"So you weren't kidding about being a gentleman," Cleo purred while stirring her drink. "What was your childhood like if you don't mind me asking?"

"Interesting," I snickered. "Both my parents were older. My dad was 73 when I was born and my mom was 49."

Now Cleo was blushing. Old parents weren't necessarily unheard of, it was just rare to meet a child of oldies. When I was young I didn't really understand what the big deal was, but it did become increasingly harder to hold onto friendships as I got older. Most sixteen-year-old boys were interested in underage drinking and panty chasing. Meanwhile I was spending my weekends going to thrift stores in search of furniture with good bones and plotting out shade gardens.

"Really?" Cleo gasped.

"Unfortunately. I've been old all my life," I admitted while poking at my pinto beans.

I even ate old. Pinto beans, smoked turkey tails, and cornbread was my favorite meal. I drank prune juice for fun. I had the nursing home diet down pat.

"No, it's not that. It's just when you said older, I was expecting like 40s or 50s. 73 kinda reminds me of Sarah and-"

"Abraham?" I interjected with a chuckle. "That was my favorite thing to call my dad before he passed."

Cleo teased me with a gentle, sentimental smile. Empathy overflowed from her warm fudge eyes.

"I'm sorry for your loss," she cooed.

"Thank you, but it's fine. I had him until he was 91. He was determined to see me graduate high school and go off to college. He basically refused to die until then. Like a stubborn ass goat," I laughed, remembering my sometimes cantankerous father.

"Tell me about your mom," Cleo said while propping her chin onto her folded hands.

She was wholly invested in whatever I had to say. My heart leapt in my chest. Just as it did the first night I met her. The sounds of clinking silverware, disconnected chatter, and scraping chairs dissolved as her syrupy giggle once again tickled my eardrums. Four days, three nights, and 14 hours was too soon to announce love of any kind, I knew that. However, even my fear of coming off as desperate and possibly black trashbag-ish couldn't stop the whisper I heard in the somewhat dark recesses of my racing mind as I watched her smile in response to my story about Saturday morning cleaning with my mother.

Cleo was mine.

I had learned that Cleo's childhood was also interesting. Her parents, once residents of Beaumont, left due to the structure of their relationship. Southern Black folks didn't really understand nor appreciate polycules. Especially not ones with two men.

"So you have two dads?" I laughed after she sheepishly explained everything. "I don't know if I'm bald enough for this. That's too spoiled."

"Oddly enough, my mom did most of my spoiling," Cleo laughed. "My dads were too sensible. Why would they buy me a pony if the neighbor down the street did pony rides for ten bucks a kid? So what if he smelled like Steel Reserve and fried bologna?"

"I'm sorry, Cleo. I have to agree with them. You can't beat a ten dollar pony ride. Them lil mfs are expensive to keep."

"Ok but listen, I had it all worked out. I was going to barter with the vets to get cheaper care bills. I'd learn how to trim hooves and put on horseshoes, and I'd pay for everything by offering my own pony rides.

They'd be five dollars more but Tulle would be in different costumes everyday and you'd smell wildflowers instead of cheap malt beer."

"You had a name picked out and everything?" I snickered.

"Oh, I had a whole business plan," Cleo nodded. "It was color coded with different shades of pink. I was really proud of that."

"You should be."

We met each other's gaze with soft laughter, then melted into a sort of stillness that reminded me of slow mornings. The kind of mornings where you just laid in bed, let your body wake up naturally, and prioritized enjoying the sun on your face. No rushing, no talking, no anxiety. Just warmth and enjoyment. Something that seemingly came easy with Cleo.

"Achm," our waiter coughed, interrupting our eye contact. "I just wanna leave this here for when you get ready."

Then he slid the black check holder between our wine glasses, placing it closer to Cleo than me. His subtle assumption annoyed me, but it annoyed me more when Cleo actually reached for it like that was something she needed to be concerned about.

"Wait, I was just going to offer to cover the tip," she protested as I snatched it from her.

"Gross, no thank you," I grumbled while pulling out my card. "I can provide for you just fine."

A stunned woman sat before me, silent and contemplative as I signed the check with a little more finesse than necessary. I had to repeatedly remind myself not to smile as she settled back into her chair and instead reached into her purse to reapply her cherry-red lipstick.

Then we feel back into a bout of intense eye contact. We probably creeped out the waitstaff with how often we stared at each other, but honestly I didn't give a fuck. People spent hours looking at the Mona Lisa and that lady was dead and gone. Cleo was a masterpiece as she lived and breathed. Why wouldn't I want to soak up as much time as possible in her presence? I knew I had technically only asked her to dinner, but I needed just a little more time with her before I said goodnight.

"Hey, rock with me for a second," I said softly.

"What's up?"

"Do you wanna go get an ice cream? I really need something sweet and there's this place not far from here that sells smores campfire cones."

"You had me at ice cream," Cleo smiled. "Lead the way."

Cleo

Before tonight, I did not think that men had the capacity to be cute. They could be cute in the face, don't get me wrong. However, they usually ruined that when they opened their mouths to speak. I knew too many men who talked themselves out of pussy because they didn't know when to shut the fuck up, especially the handsome ones.

But then there was Mars.

He was cute, and not just because he was handsome, but because he was nervous and genuine, and all the good things that reminded me that we were just humans trying to make the best out of short lives on this floating rock. His throat bobbed when I kissed his cheek as a thanks for dinner, he blushed when I reached for his hand as we walked the short trip to the ice cream shop, and he blabbered over his words if I stared at him too long.

You know, that cute shit you do when you really liked someone.

"What are you having?" he asked while bringing his hands to my shoulders to warm me up.

If we weren't in public, I probably would've leaned into his touch and buried myself in his herby, soapy scent. However I couldn't lose focus. There was a massive menu of at least forty different offerings in front of me, and despite the mountain of choices, I zeroed in on my selections almost immediately.

"A medium cup. Smores on the bottom, maple bacon on the top, with caramel drizzle and chocolate sprinkles."

Mars' entire face scrunched up as he considered my choices. I could practically hear the "unn" going off in his head when I asked for maple bacon, but he ordered and paid for it with no questions asked.

"I don't think I've ever seen someone order sprinkles," Mars whispered as we sat down with our cups. "I genuinely thought they were for decoration only."

"Ohhhh that's why your face did that. I thought it was because of the maple bacon."

"No, no," Mars clarified. "I can rock with a lil salty and sweet. What I can't rock with is sprinkles. They don't even taste like anything."

"It's the texture," I sighed. "It adds a little crunch."

"Cookies do the same thing," he argued with a head shake. "Everyone loves cookies. Except for the weird, pretty lady who orders edible pebbles instead."

"Look!" I whisper-shouted as a family picked up their order behind us. "She has sprinkles."

There was a little brown-skinned girl reaching on her tiptoes to grab her cup off the counter. A smattering of rainbow-colored sprinkles rolled down the vanilla hill and straight into her mouth with her jerky movements, and she smiled despite her mom chastising her about eating without a spoon.

"She's like four!" Mars roared in a fit of laughter. "That's allowed."

"Okay! And I'm only thirty-four," I protested with a pout. "We're practically the same age."

"If that's the case, I'm about to call the police on myself," he replied quietly. "And I want them to check the hard drives."

"Shutup," I giggled while pushing his shoulder.

Mars' body gave way to my playful shove, but I could feel the solid muscle hiding under his thermal. It was corded and rippling with every gentle movement. Especially when he laughed at the little ballerina besides us. My sprinkle sorority sister was twirling on the tips of her toes between her parents, singing a song of appreciation.

"She's so freaking cute," Mars whispered.

He had a look of pure adoration on his face while he waved to her, and instead of my coochie weeping over the perfect potential father in front of me, I was thrown into an immediate panic.

"Tonight is going great, but there's something I have to tell you!" I blurted out.

I really liked Mars, but I had my dealbreakers and I was sure he had his. I learned early on that it was best to announce them in the beginning, although I had forgotten this time around because the night was going so well. Considerate men were a double-edged sword. Safety and comfort came too easily when dealing with them.

"Fuck," Mars frowned as his attention snapped back to me. "Are you married, Cleo? Is that what you're about to tell me?"

"What, negro?" I grimaced, scrunching up my nose. "Why would you think that?"

"I don't know," he shrugged. "You're very pretty so it's not unfathomable, and to be honest I've had it happen like that before."

While I desperately wanted to know more about that last little tidbit, my dried-up ovaries were busy reminding me to tell him the truth before we got too deep into this and I ended up hurt.

"Listen Mars, I like you a lot and I'm excruciatingly single, but I need you to know I don't want kids. I love kids. I like educating them and supporting them, I just don't want to birth nor raise them."

"Oh, ok," he nodded before returning to his ice cream.

This was the second time tonight something he said had stunned me into silence. I was quiet after the bill mostly because I feared if I opened my mouth, I might accidentally end up putting his dick in it. Now however, I was shocked at his acceptance. I expected the normal fuss and hubbub that came with such an announcement. I even had a whole speech prepared in case he asked me if I was really sure.

"Ok?" I asked, dumfounded. "That's it?"

"Yeah, unless you wanna talk about it more? I don't want kids either. I like sleeping in and taking long vacations too much. Plus my best friend has five so I get my uncle fix that way," Mars explained.

"Oh," I said, my voice nearly phantom.

My voice wobbled under his gaze because when he grinned, I heard the trumpets of heaven's gate. Tears nearly started flowing. Mars checked every box on my "impossible" list and then some. Love was crazy after only four days of light conversation and dinner, but I knew that it would come fast and hard.

"You got something there," he grumbled, breaking me out of my trance.

He gently cupped my chin with his big hand before lazily swiping across my cheek with his thumb to collect some misplaced ice cream. As embarrassing as it was, I was a messy eater by nature. But the least I could do was hand him a wet napkin to clean his hands.

However Mars didn't need it.

Because instead he instinctively brought his thumb to his mouth to suck it clean. Full lips parted just slightly to show off an artfully rolled tongue, a deft tongue that left behind no trace of my mess on his brown skin. That dangerous grin overloaded my senses once he was done, and I found myself clinging to his arm, watching every crease, crinkle, and dimple his smile produced.

"The maple bacon is actually nice. I've been coming here for years and I never would've tried it," he said casually as he pushed the hair from my eyes.

"Yeah," I whispered with an entranced nod. "The savory sweet really works well."

"Mhm," he agreed while once again cupping my chin.

He tipped my head upward just slightly so that my eyes could meet his and then I watched in awe as his entire body relaxed. If I didn't know any better, I'd assume he'd been tranquilized by an ass dart or some shit, but Mars had been looking at me like I was the 10th wonder of the world all evening. It was both refreshing and terrifying because I was 100% certain he was going to ruin my life. Especially when his brows furrowed in contemplation as he asked,

"Would you like to do this again, Cleo?"

"Yes," I whispered, knowing that this was likely the last first date I'd ever have. "I'd like that very much."

Homecoming

Mars-9 months later

"Get your shit and get out!" I growled.

"You just want me to leave so you can fuck your girlfriend when she gets back in town."

"Yeah, and also because you're sweating up my brand new couch. This velvet is for love, not whores."

I had the same best friend I had at age eight. Jack James was a tall, lanky, Pisces and also a victim of an old father. We bonded over that in addition to our love of music and food. He'd been my Ace for almost three decades so I didn't care if he had to crash here after doing it up on a kid-free night, but Cleo was coming back from a three week trip and I was practically itching to hold her. Friendship aside, I was a man in love.

"Whatever," Jack chuckled. "I got a party to get ready for anyway. Don-"

"Don't worry, I won't forget the rum punch. Now get out. I gotta pick Cleo up in 40 minutes and the couch smells like the sweat of a drunkard."

"Yeah, yeah. Just tell Miss Cleo I said heyyyyy and I'm still available," he teased.

There weren't many things I regretted, but telling Jack that Cleo was a private tutor was one of them. She now tutored one of his daughters and he took every opportunity to remind me that he had a thing for teachers. He was still in love with his ex-wife so I knew he wasn't serious, but the possessive goblin in me made me wanna trip his hoe ass about Cleo.

"Jay Jay, please don't make me beat your ass before lunch," I sighed.

"I wouldn't dream of it sunshine," he grinned while twisting the knob. "Now go get our wife. The girls miss her."

He ducked out the door, only narrowly avoiding being hit with my workboot. I could hear his laughter ring out as he skipped across the lawn and I had half a mind to run after him, but then my alarm sounded, reminding me to get my ass to the airport.

My vindictive tendencies would have to wait.

Cleo

I had never been so happy to be back on American soil. Three weeks didn't seem like that long of a trip in the grand scheme of things, but there I was jogging through the airport, my titties practically slapping against my chin, all to get back to Mars.

Love was so stupid.

I was running and no one was chasing me. Not only was that Black blasphemy, it was also personally unheard of. I hadn't run to meet a man since I was seven and those men were my dads. Yet when I saw the cherry red Mercedes with the popped trunk in the pickup lane, I sprinted.

"Oh, Cleo," Mars purred as he caught me in a spinning hug. "I missed you so much, Mamas,"

My feet were back on the ground but I couldn't be bothered to let him go and move out of them people's way just yet.

"I missed you too," I nearly sobbed. "Next time you just gotta fit in my suitcase."

"Don't tempt me," he murmured while rubbing my back.

I started to sway in contentment until a car honked behind us, reminding me that we were unfortunately in public. Yeah we were being annoying with our PDA, but that didn't stop me from slipping the offender the bird as he passed in his lil raggedy ass Pontiac. Folks were allowed to enjoy being in love. Even his, "salute the general" hairline ass.

"Ok, bring yo mean ass on," Mars chuckled while forcing my eyebrows apart. "I got breakfast coming to the house."

Mars lived in Lakeview, 40 minutes away from the airport. I was used to the drive now, but I remembered how nervous I was the first time. Mostly because Luci reminded me that the lakes surrounding his house probably had bodies in them after she googled his address. Today I was 99% sure that Mars wasn't a serial killer who dug watery graves, but I was still nervous on the drive over for whatever reason.

Maybe it was because Mars was humming along to Fortunate while his greedy hand squeezed and caressed my left thigh. If he wasn't driving I was sure that he would've been rubbing on me like a cat in heat and I would've done the same. I had been gone for one week fewer than the last time we had sex. Auntie Flo visited the week before I left, only to leave as soon as I boarded my 8pm flight.

I was pissed off about that up until 1 hour ago.

Now though I was nervous, because he was such a tease. He wouldn't say it out loud, but he would do everything in his power to make me lose my mind before he lost his. Mars liked the long game, especially the chase. Which is why he didn't complain once about us not having sex until month two. He had a plan, he just needed a platform, a blindfold, and a little ribbon.

"Did you really miss me, or did you just miss folding me like a sheet?" I asked, ejecting my lip just slightly.

"Why can't it be both?" Mars chuckled. "I miss playing in it, but I miss your corny jokes more."

"They're not corny!" I argued. "I swear I was a comedian in another life."

"Yeah but in this life, they're a little corny, Mamas. That's ok though because my favorite chips are Fritos."

My mouth unhinged like a surprised snake. Did this man really just compare my sense of humor to the worst bag of chips in the variety pack? I didn't know which to be mad at more. The fact that he was grinning like a Cheshire cat, or the fact that it got a snicker out of me.

"Please stop talking to me," I huffed.

"Fine," Mars shrugged before queuing up his oldies playlist. "I'll just sing to you instead."

The leaves had only just begun to change in Texas, and there were big Mars-high piles of them gathered all over the front yard. He'd kept himself busy while I was gone. The porch and pillars had a fresh coat of paint, the beds were re-mulched, and the door was decorated for Halloween. The house was also spotless when we got back. Mars was a firm believer of bleach and Pinesol. So much so that you could often smell it from the steps. It could singe your nose hairs some days, but it was welcome after being in funky ass Paris for three weeks. The scent of brown sugar and peppercorn bacon was also welcome after my ten hour flight and 20 minute mobile concert. Europe had good bread, but I missed cheese grits and hard-fried potatoes.

"Ugh, it's so good to be home," I groaned as I reached to untie my boots.

"It's good to have you home," Mars replied while taking my hand so I could use him for balance.

I closed my eyes and let my feet curl into the freshly vacuumed carpet once my boots popped off. Mars left me to decompress in peace, but the sounds of him shuffling about, unzipping everything and washing whatever clothing I had in my luggage while fussing about the obnoxious smell of lingering tobacco made me smile.

Cigarette smoke was one of his biggest pet peeves, and one of the few things that would make him cuss. Every Thursday evening after tutoring, he would immediately wash everything I had on. My client, or rather my client's parents, were big smokers, something Mars and I detested since we both had the PTC gene. If Holly wasn't up for the Olympics I would've turned down their travel request for that alone, but the kid had grown on me and Mars promised he could suck it up. I guess he meant the trip, not the smell.

"I just need to take this damn bra off," I sighed as my nerves finally relaxed.

The first three clasps popped with no issue, but the fourth was stubborn and twisted, digging back into position like a thorn. I let out a ragged whimper that summoned Mars to my side in an instant.

"May I?" he asked, drawing all his breath into a soothing hum.

I nodded then collapsed against his chest, allowing him full scope of my back.

He was quick at first. He knew I didn't like to be in Bras once I got home, so he wasted no time freeing me from that last, stubborn bent clasp. However once that was done he slowed to a syrupy pace. Something that was unhurried and all consuming as he traced the length of my spine.

"You never answered my question, Cleo." he growled while lifting the hem of my shirt.

I jumped at the searing sensation of his fingertips dragging over my bristled skin. My eyes dilated to see the man in front of me in vivid color, and my nipples tightened against the thin wool sweater I wore, threatening to poke right through the weave if we continued. Yet Mars remained unmoved as I pressed my hips into his.

He was so hard that I could practically cum just like that if he let me, but he was too serious about his question to appreciate the situation.

"What question, Mars?" I huffed, as I rocked against him impatiently.

Quickly, his hands left my back and came up to settle in the loose curls hanging on either side of my head. His fingertips rubbed small circles into my scalp while he repositioned my head.

"May I?" he asked again, this time grazing his lips against mine.

The tentative kiss taunted all my sensibilities. The blinds were wide open, but if he kissed me how I wanted to be kissed then and there, I'd happily put on a show. I chased his lips only for him to pull away before I could capture them. He gave me a patient smile as he waited for the answer.

The answer to his favorite question.

"Please," I gulped, giving him the permission he sought.

I was pressed against him in an instant, feet dangling off the floor, with the curve of my back being supported by his left arm. His thick, coarse beard teased my collarbone as he peppered my neck and throat in wet kisses, while I teased his earlobe with my canines.

"I'm so glad you're home," Mars groaned while pulling my legs around his waist.

"Me too," I sighed.

My greedy hands squeezed his pecs with abandon as he kissed down the curve of my neck. God, I loved meaty men. Especially mine. I would happily pass out from the lack of air so long as he kept his mouth on me, and this time I almost did. Kiss after kiss left me a dizzy, breathless mess as we walked backward onto the couch. Them Mars forced our separation by flopping down.

"I love seeing you on top of me like this," he grinned.

The proof was in his pants as he spread his legs to better accommodate the width of my ass. Then once we were comfortable, he slid his thumbs underneath the sides of my belly and bounced me a few times for good measure.

"You gone make me ride this time?" I whined.

It's not that I minded riding, especially when I was ovulation feral and fresh off a shift. I just needed something else right now. Something like weight, heat, and sweet surrender while I got pounded into the cushions.

"No, Mamas," he grinned. "I know what you need. I just wanted to enjoy the view first."

I was about to ask what he meant by that before he pulled my shirt over my head, allowing my newly freed breasts to spill into his mouth. My mind had been in shambles ever since Mars showed me what his tongue was capable of on our first date, and moments like this only worsened my mental condition.

His nimble tongue was an expert at my unraveling as he traced my dinner-plate areolas and tugged at my sensitive nipples with the tips of his canines. I had back breaking E cups, but Mars was always determined to fit an entire tit in his mouth, if not both.

"Greedy," I hissed as he nipped me.

A low, rumbly laugh shook through me as Mars widened his jaw to kiss it better.

His lips were the perfect pillows to soothe the gentle bites before he swallowed me whole again. It was too much, and the reminder that my pussy was hollow became more pressing each second.

"Fuck me or leave me alone," I demanded when the pulse between my legs became too intense.

Mars snapped forward with a scowl, and I scowled back. I loved my boyfriend, but there was a month's worth of frustration pooling in my lower belly. Then there he was looking all fine in his plaid button down like a cornbread-fed lumberjack. All thick and handsome in his plaid and bootcut denim. I needed him to swing that wood my way, and quickly.

"Pretty girl, did we leave our manners back in Paris?" Mars cooed while scratching my scalp.

Cats had the right idea. I'd domesticate myself too if I was regularly getting scratched like this. He knew just how to get me. My head dipped between my shoulders as I relaxed into his touch. Attitude? Evaporated. Act right? Reactivated.

I groaned as his fingertips loosened my thick curls. Three weeks of schoolmarm buns made me forget what it felt like to have air on my scalp. It felt almost as good as sex. *Almost.*

"Let's try that again," he said, removing his touch.

"Please," I whimpered, pushing my lips into a pout. "I'm asking nicely."

"There we go, Mamas," Mars cooed while rolling on top of me. "That's what I like to hear."

He rewarded my good manners by loosening the brass buckle securing his pants, and then tending to my creased and wrinkled slacks.

"I see Fat Ma has her winter mink on," Mars chuckled while ridding me of my panties.

He started to play with the tight coils adorning my snatch, completely ignoring my swollen clit that was practically begging for attention. I would've been annoyed but he seemed so delighted with the crop of fuzz. I was almost happy that I accidentally forgot my clippers stateside.

"It was almost impossible to get a wax appointment in Paris," I pouted.

"Oh believe me, I'm not complaining. I love your curls as above and so below."

I had a joke about the catacombs, but Mars interrupted me when his head dipped down, eager to show me just how much he loved it. First by rubbing his nose in it, and then by showering it in sloppy kisses.

"Fuck," I hissed as he pulled my legs onto his shoulders.

His tongue parted my slit like Moses parting the red sea, allowing his lips to latch on to the tight bundle of nerves hiding underneath it. His licks were slow but hungry, and the way he grunted while eating it made me realize why I was pissed off the whole three weeks I was in Paris.

It was because I didn't have him there with me to eat me like a chocolate croissant.

My heart rate climbed with the increasing pleasure, eventually reaching a summit that I had no choice but to freefall from. Mars held my hips to keep me in rhythm as I bucked against his eager mouth. Stars dotted my vision as I relished the sensation of his slightly rough hands roving all over the globes of my ass, and my voice rang out in a pitch that you damn near needed a radio to hear. My back arched off the couch, a physical acknowledgement of his skills, while my legs shook like newly separated tectonic plates. My first nut after four weeks of abstaining was a doozy. It took ages for my spirit to return to its vessel and the post release buzz felt so good I almost didn't want it to. However, once I was done convulsing like a freshly exorcised body, Mars' tongue slid down to clean my cum off my twitching asshole.

"God, you so fuckin nasty," I groaned when I noticed his hand squeezing his shaft. "Eating it like this should be illegal."

He peeked over the rim of his now-steamed up glasses to shoot me a deviant smile before returning to his meal. Knowing the state of Texas, it probably was illegal.

Not that Mars gave a fuck.

If I didn't push his head away after nutting so hard that my legs gave out, he would eat me until the next morning. He didn't give a damn about sleep, actual food, or a job as long as there was pussy in his face. Lockjaw feared him, and rightfully so.

"Wipe your face," I moaned as slid off his shirt. "You got cum in your beard."

"I'm aware," Mars smiled while peeling off his button down and tabling his glasses. "Even though I would've liked to save it for later."

His tattooed arms almost distracted me from the nightmare of his suggestion. Green ink made up a good deal of his gothic work. Especially the wild-eyed cryptids. I was hypnotized by the way the grim reaper's scythe hugged his forearm when he stretched his arms overhead to remove his A-shirt. However the shine on his face brought me back to Earth. I would rather die than show up with my man to his best friend's party with him looking like an iced Honey Bun.

"Mars," I chided as he began to crawl back on the couch. "Clean your face."

"Fine."

He reluctantly wiped his face on one of his discarded shirts before tossing it in the hamper and rejoining me.

"Can I please fuck you now?" he asked while thumbing my lower lip. "Please," I nodded while aligning his tip with my entrance.

A less reverent man would've just rammed into me, letting his frustration triumph in the moment. However Mars was no amateur. He pressed forward slowly, taking time to appreciate the greedy way in which my pussy sucked him inside while I appreciated the veins stretching across his width. A smile crept across his face inch-by-inch until he bottomed out, and the most wicked, seductive moan crept from his throat when we finally settled.

"Cleooooo," he whined. "God I missed you, baby."

I melted into the cushions as Mars' arms came around my waist, holding me tight and still so he could stretch me open. That part was necessary because otherwise my impatient ass would've forced his hips down. Which meant writing a check that I knew I couldn't cash.

"Mars," I sighed as he kissed me.

My hands came to his shoulders to pull him closer, encouraging his head to dip into the space between my shoulder and my ear. Obsessive men sounded good in theory, but what happened when your man's dick got even harder just because he smelled your skin? Well, me being the gluttonous wanch I was, I greedily lifted my hips to accept as much as he would give me. Mars was easy, so he happily stuffed me until my knees were resting on my shoulders.

"It's so fucking good," he moaned with his warm spearmint breath tickling the shell of my ear. "Fuck, Cleo. I love you."

"I can tell," I whined while rolling my hips to fuck him back.

And I could, especially during days like this.

Mars didn't have sex for practically sake. Instead he treated sex like an art form, making sure to paint a picture with every exaggerated movement and ragged moan. It was one of the few times he let himself be as dramatic and as thorough as he wanted to be. Which is why we almost always made love. Honestly, I didn't really understand the concept of making love in my twenties and early thirties. To me it sounded like regular ole fucking except slower. However since being with Mars, I understood that the pace was the point. The soft kisses that you could only get with a two-step beat, the unapologetic moans and the unhurried pleasure, the roving touches that made you realize that you like having your navel traced, and the orgasms that came about after all of that while you looked the love of your life in the eye. That was the point.

"Welcome home," Mars rasped in between soft pecks.

"Thanks baby," I squeaked back.

He chuckled at my faded, cracking voice before easing out of me. I sounded like I belonged on one of those commercials with the ex-models who used to smoke a carton a day, but that wasn't anything that couldn't be soothed with tea.

"That's a big mess," Mars sighed. "A month is too long, Mamas. You know I get sensitive."

"Why are you saying that like it's my fault?"

"Because it is. Your fast ass locked me in with those thick ass thighs. Now look at us."

Ok, so maybe I did get a little carried away. I didn't thinking wrapping my legs around his hips would spell immediate doom, but I didn't regret that it did. I was happy, relaxed, and full of cum.

"You're trouble," Mars yawned as he pulled me onto his chest.

"Uhuh."

He said that frequently, as if he wasn't the reason we were to begin with. I just wanted some spices that night, but all it took was one smile for me to leave with a boyfriend.

"I'll be right back."

He climbed off the cushion in a struggling heap, leaving me alone in my warm and gooey post-coital haze. Soon jetlag caught up and settled into my achy bones. However right before my eyes fluttered close, Mars returned and scooped me off the couch.

"Where are we going?" I groaned while throwing my arms around his neck.

Mars didn't respond, which was fine because I was used to him occasionally going mute. He grew up in a house with four older sisters so sometimes silence was his default. Plus even without knowing all the details, I knew we weren't going far. I was butt ass naked and Mars was both paranoid and possessive. He hated that I left all the curtains open at my apartment because I was almost never dressed, and somehow he had convinced himself that someone other than him was checking for me. I guess that's why all the curtains in his house were drawn shut at 3:30 in the afternoon. Honestly, I wasn't complaining about that either because I was still tired. The darkness was keeping a headache at bay, and that coupled with the soft sounds of his heavy bare feet padding against the hardwood started to lure me back to sleep.

"No bueno," he exclaimed while softly rubbing my back. "You can sleep after I wash your hair."

I was returned to the floor in the primary bathroom, where steam rose out of the soaker tub. The water was tinted an irresistible shade of violet while small flowers floated about. It looked like fairy soup, and I was about to ask him what it was, but then I realized the air around us smelled like Sugarplum Bliss bath bombs, a favorite of mine for the last decade or so. What Megan say? My man, my man, my man! Yeah, he took his title seriously.

"Mars," I cooed while pecking him. "Do you love me or something?"

"Cleo, you know I adore you," he sighed as he placed a kiss on my temple.

Yeah, I knew and not just because Luci announced it randomly in the middle of us talking one day. I knew it from the very first time we kissed. Feeling sparks was one thing, but I felt us click. It was like gears sliding in place to make a clock tick. Commitment usually terrified me, but it was a done deal after that. Now we were almost a year in and I had absolutely no regrets handing over my heart to the myth called Mars.

Fifteen minutes later, I was sitting in Mars' lap, humming along to Free Nationals and sipping wine as he gingerly separated my curls. Once finger combed, we moved onto tackling remaining kinks with a wide tooth comb, and finally a wet brush before they were twisted out of the way.

"Was the water hard?" he asked while detangling another section of hair.

"Extremely," I frowned. "I went through an unethical amount of leave in."

"I can tell," Mars tsked. "You got a little breakage on the ends from the dryness."

"Will you clip my ends?"

"I'll do it next time we blow dry your hair. For now let's just focus on repairing your moisture barrier. It's minimal so I think I can hide it."

Most people who met me assumed that my hair was maintained by some uppity, bougie, celebrity stylist who cost thousands of dollars a month when in reality, it was the handiwork of my boyfriend. His Mama was an old school beautician who used Marcel irons and did a mean roller set, and Mars picked up a lot of good tips from her. Then he went and decided to use his GI bill to attend cosmetology school, before ultimately deciding to become an electrician like his late father. That was a wild career shift, but they both made a lot of sense based on what kind of person Mars was. Creative, curious, but also logical and approach based. All things he attributed to his unique "old" upbringing. I had to agree with him most days.

Both his parents were long gone but I hoped they knew that they raised a good man.

Jokes & Mirrors

Mars

They said distance makes the heart grow fonder, but all distance did for me was make me a clingy mess. I could've easily spent all day in bed with Cleo, squeezing her, smelling her, and tracing all the cushy hills and valleys that I loved so much, but I just had to agree to bring rum punch. Now I was out of bed, putting on both a costume and a mask so I wouldn't be branded as a bad friend.

Although I would still kinda be a bad friend because we were definitely leaving early.

"I'm so glad the year is almost over," I whispered while nuzzling Cleo's fresh curls. "I'm tired of sharing you."

"Sharing me with who?" Cleo chuckled. "Jay's basically your family."

"My point still stands."

"Hey, so that reminds me," she said while spinning around.

I was desperately trying to school my face, but for whatever reason Cleo's segue made my stomach lurch. Not for any particular reason.

My paranoia was just acting up, and the little voice in the back of my head told me this would be bad.

"I know I was supposed to meet your family over Thanksgiving, but would it be ok if we did Christmas instead? My grandma reached out to me last week and asked if I could make theirs since I missed last year," Cleo explained.

"Oh, ok. That's fine," I nodded.

Was it fine though?

Eh.

I loved Cleo's parents and I talked with them often, however, the things I heard about her extended family were not good. They seemed judgmental and rude to the point that no one had bothered to keep in touch with Cleo or her siblings all these years because of her parents relationship. Not even this grandma she was so excited to finally meet. Hell, she'd been living in Beaumont for a year and they still hadn't physically checked on her. As soon as they heard she had a man they were satisfied. Which was blowing me because I could've been any-body. They didn't even check to see if I was employed.

I mean I kept a job, but it was the principle. I could've been a bum!

"Oh my God, Mars," she gasped. "You look like you smelled shit." I finally realized that despite trying to be cool about it, I had my face balled up like Kerry Washington. Just all kinds of stank. Lip twitching and everything.

"I'm sorry," I offered. "I think I'm just nervous for you. I know you really want to build a relationship with them."

And personally, I didn't think they were worth building a relationship with. However I'd keep my cynicism to myself for now. I ain't know them people from a can of paint and it wasn't my job to tell her to avoid. I just had to be there for her in the event that shit went left.

"Thank you for being a good sport," she cooed. "I'll make you a personal pan of cornbread that day to make up for it."

I was simple and Cleo knew it, because I was cheesing like a fool at the mere mention of fresh cornbread. Cleo's cornbread was the definition of country cooking. She used buttermilk and brown sugar, and she only ever made it in a cast iron pan. It reminded me of my sister's, but better. Yes I was wary of them folks, but I was like a guard dog being distracted with a fresh cut of steak.

"Can we just skip this party and I eat cornbread off your titties tonight?" I pouted.

"No sir," Cleo waved before slipping into her shoes. "Now grab those pitchers. We're already technically late."

The party was in full effect by the time we made it to Sugarland. The girls were twenty miles away with Jay's mom for the weekend, and he was bringing a whole new meaning to kid free. It looked like an old school MTV video shoot with women dancing topless on the balconies, bass shaking the windows, and niggas shooting dice on the porch.

"Oh shit you made it!" Jay cheered as we cut through the living room. "Not gonna lie, I thought Miss Foxy Cleo would've had you comatose with your dick out like last time."

"Man, would you shut up!" I hissed as I threw one of the pitchers into his hand.

Cleo was ovulating the first time we had sex. She came home after two rounds of bottomless mimosas, with low hooded eyes, and her panties stuffed into her purse. I thought I had everything under control because my last sperm analysis read zero and there was Powerade stocked in the fridge, but then I woke up not knowing what day it was while Jay's ass was hooting and hollering in my living room.

Apparently I had been asleep for fourteen hours straight and Cleo was concerned when she couldn't wake me up that morning before she went to work.

Unfortunately she called that mother fucker.

"I'm just saying," he shrugged while popping an appetizer into his mouth. "History does repeat itself."

"Oh what's that?" Cleo exclaimed.

She was still hungry after devouring brunch, which made sense considering that we also got rounds two and three in between the tub and the kitchen respectively. I almost stopped for tacos just to hold her over, but she was adamant that Jay's bougie ass had good catered food waiting on us.

As usual, she was right.

"Jalapeno and lobster Rangoon," Jay answered while getting her a clean plate. "Help yourself, lady. I'm about to borrow your boyfriend's muscles real quick."

Speaking of history repeating itself...

Me and Jay quickly set up the punch pitchers and then hurried off to his office. We had about ten minutes before Cleo finished setting up her plate and came looking for us, and this was not how I wanted her to catch me. Funny enough, me and Jay were in this same situation twelve years earlier, only the roles were reversed.

"Where are you gonna put it?" Jay asked in a whisper. "Do you even have pockets on that thing?"

To answer the question, no. My Garfield costume did not have pockets. It was also a snug fit so I couldn't wear jeans under it. I ended up having to borrow a pair of Cleo's yoga pants, which surprise surprise, also did not have pockets. Women's clothing infuriated me to no end and I often thought about learning how to sew just so I could fix Cleo's shit. Tonight had only intensified that urge.

"I'm just gonna put it in my underwear," I shrugged nonchalantly.

"In your underwear!?" Jay hollered. "You're gonna have it rubbing against your sweaty ass balls all night?"

"Aye, it's in a box!"

"I can just drop it off later," Jay suggested, his face twisted with disgust.

I could tell he was seriously considering holding my shit hostage, and that simply wouldn't do. Jay was easily distracted. He was especially liable for fuckery if his ex-wifed popped up. I loved Sharonda, but her timing was always piss poor. I couldn't risk not hearing from Jay for a month while he had my shit once she decided to get sentimental about the holidays.

"Nigga, if you don't give me my ring!"

"Ok, ok!" he said, finally surrendering. "But if she wrinkles her nose after saying yes, don't say I didn't warn you."

I snatched the box from him before quickly giving the ring inside a once over. From the platinum double band, to the large garnet set in the center, and the inscription I hoped Cleo would occasionally run her fingertips over. Everything about it perfectly complimented the beauty of the woman it would soon belong to. It took two months for my jeweler to set everything just right, and it was well worth the wait.

"Still aiming for a month?"

"Two," I corrected. "Gonna let the holidays blow over first. She's meeting her Dad's side this Thanksgiving."

"Eh," Jay cringed. "Have they even checked on her since she's been down here?"

"That's the same thing I said, but hey. Hope for the best, prepare for the worst."

"A word. I'm sure you'll have her so thankful even if things don't work out."

I cut my eyes at this grinning ass fool as a warning, and instead of shaping up, he decided to make the hand gesture to really nail his point home. Technically he wasn't wrong, but I was too much of a secretive prude to continue this conversation. Some things were just for me to know. Cleo turning me into a fiend was one of them.

"I'm leaving. I refuse to talk about my sex life with you."

"Why not!?" Jay called as I rejoined the party. "I already know it's good!"

"Goodbye, Jack!"

Cleo

Somehow I had lost my fat cat.

Not Big Pearl who was between my legs, but my grouchy boyfriend who was dressed as America's favorite psychopath. He was fussing at Jay's nosey butt one minute, and he had vanished in the next. How I lost a six foot tall, bearded, Black man dressed as Garfield was beyond me, but truthfully, I knew I was distracted by the snacks.

"Are you dressed as a pan of lasagna?" a woman asked.

I had to do a double take when I turned around cause we looked eerily similar. We were the same height, the same complexion, and we even had a mole in the same spot. Right in the middle of our chin. She was just less hippy and busty than me, and honestly I envied her for it. My back creaked every morning.

"Yes. It's part of a couple's costume," I explained.

"Wait, is your boyfriend Garfield?"

"Yeah?"

"He's looking for you out back by the pie station."

"There's a pie station?" I gasped.

It was embarrassing how quickly that information distracted me. But on the flip side, it was crazy how well Mars knew me. Because had I known there was a pie station, that's exactly where I would've been posted up.

"Come on, I'll show you," the lady dressed as Fairy Godmotha Whitney Houston offered.

"Ok. I'm Cleopatricia by the way."

"Cleopatricia, that sounds oddly familiar. I'm Janae."

"I'm not sure why," I shrugged. "I don't really get out much, but I do tutor Lina, Jay's oldest."

"Ooh yeah. Maybe that's it," Janae nodded. "I usually braid the girl's hair. I try to keep up with everything they talk about, but sometimes all I can remember are names."

Yeah that was fair. Lina made the most sense at eleven and even her storytelling left me lost at times. I wasn't sure if her three-year-old sister Chloe was speaking English half the time.

"Same," I nodded.

"Are y'all twins?" someone asked as we walked onto the back patio. Janae laughed it off but I was seconds away from texting my dad and making him explain my bubbly Doppleganger.

"No we just met!" she giggled before pulling me along. "I wonder why people keep saying that. I get we're both short."

"I think it's a little more to our similarities than our height."

"Really?" she asked, tilting her head to the side the same way I did.

God it was creepy. My heart skipped a little when our eyes locked. I almost wanted to run.

Before I could though, Mars skipped up to us with a plate of pie samplings in hand. Only to stop dead in his tracks when he saw Janae.

"Y'all look scarily alike," he gulped. "Cleo, are you sure your dad hasn't been back in Beaumont within the last thirty or so years?"

"Positive," I nodded.

"It's probably just a coincidence," Janae shrugged. "Maybe both our ancestors came from the same tribe. DNA is tricky like that."

"I guess," Mars replied cautiously. "Anyway, I see you've met Janae. Cleo, this is Janae, my youngest cousin. Janae, this is my Cleo."

"Ohhhh, that's why you sound so familiar," Janae gasped. "Mars doesn't shut up about you. I should've put that together when I saw the costumes earlier."

Then she taped her temple in thought, which bless her heart, she appeared not to have many of.

"Thank you for bringing Cleo to me in one piece, Nae," Mars said appreciatively. "However, we're about to make like a chip and dip. This is kinda weirding me out."

"Fair enough," Janae nodded as she swayed in the warmth of the fire pit. "I wouldn't want my lover to remind me of my cousin either. It would make orgasms very awkward."

"Lord, hammercy," Mars mumbled while staring at the ground instead of us. "Bye, Nae. See you in a few weeks for Thanksgiving."

"Bye, Chewy! Bye, twinnem!" she waved.

Mars bristled beside me, his back going ram rod straight as he passed quick glances between myself and his cousin. I had no doubts that Janae's orgasm comment was stuck in his head, especially since my multitude of expressions were still fresh in his memory.

"I had a joke about wanting to eat some lasagna, but she ruined it," he scowled.

"Oh, baby. Let's get you some actual food to soothe the pain of your forfeiture," I offered.

"Fine," Mars sighed while kicking the grass. "As long as you put your booty on me when they start playing The Ying Yang Twins."

"Deal."

Trust Fall

Mars

God, I loved sexing Cleo. She was so soft, so reactive, so addicting. Hearing her voice soften under my efforts constantly rewired my brain. Especially when I hit her favorite spot and she sang my name. The melody was perfect as she stretched out the two syllables in my name to make them sound larger than life. And I'm sure God was jealous of her anointing hymn, as even the angels would have trouble reproducing it.

If I could live inside of her, I would. I spent most of my days thinking about growing old with her on a plot of land that was filled with all her favorite flowers.

I didn't think I could be any deeper in love.

But then she would grin, drag her fingers up my arm, and whisper seductive secrets that were only meant for me as her sharp teeth nipped the edge of my ear.

Cleopatricia King had me spinning.

"You know you're mine, right?" I panted as I pumped into her slow and deep.

Cleo's slick sex fluttered around me as I did, enthusiastically welcoming me home. Some distance usually gave my stamina a boost, but I collapsed against her despite my original hopes of going all night, needing to feel all of her.

Fuck, I was hopeless.

"I know," Cleo gasped as her hands explored my back.

Her warm fingertips traced over the lines of my tattoos and the cords of my muscles until I became putty in her hands, a machine that only she could utilize. My hips flowed into hers according to her chosen rhythm, a steady rock that was sure to slowly induce madness between both parties.

"Cleo," I groaned as I buried my free hand in her curls.

I could still taste her on my breath as it passed over my lips. Sweet and musky, a balance that left me craving more. I had half a mind to go back for one more taste, but the clever woman brought her hands around my shoulders and her legs around my hips to lock me in place. Her skin was soft and warm, slicked with sweat, and scented with Brown Sugar. I could practically taste it every time we kissed, and that in itself was overwhelming until her airy voice grounded me.

"Mars."

She spoke my name with reverence before pulling me into a kiss that left me breathless. Then another, and a few more until I was so dizzy and overstimulated that I could hardly think. Our strokes accelerated and my stomach tightened with the need to release. I wasn't Superman. I knew all those tender kisses would eventually get the best of me.

But first I needed her to say it.

"Tell me," I growled while grabbing a handful of her curves.

Her soft flesh spilled over my hands as she cried out, telling me something incoherent. I realized then that my instructions were unclear.

"Tell me you're mine," I whimpered, my voice growing soft.

The logical part of me knew she was mine wholly and unquestionably, but I needed to hear it. I needed to know that I wasn't in this alone.

"I'm yours, Mars," Cleo panted as she pressed her lips against mine.

I shivered as her pointed nails dragged up the sensitive skin of my back to pull me further into her vortex. Yet I didn't fight it. We synced further under her direction, falling into a frenzied, reckless rhythm that would undoubtedly end me. But I couldn't care less.

She was mine. Cleo was mine.

The confirmation repeated in my mind ten fold until the overwhelming notion raced down my spine and settled into my stomach. Then I had the urge to bring her closer. Into my lap and against my racing heart.

"Fuck, fuck, fuck. Baby, fuck!" I yelled as I picked her up.

I wrapped my arms around her thick waist and began pounding into her like a rutting dog. Her smoldering, over-sexed eyes remained low while we pushed each other off the edge, until they coaxed a smile from me as she separated part of my tormented soul from my body. A smile that was present even when my eyes went out of focus.

"What the fuck did you do to me, pretty girl?" I groaned as I shook from the last of my release.

I was too tired to hold my head up, and yet when Cleo drew her lips into a seductive smile I found the energy to meet her pensive eyes.

"I love you," she sighed.

"I love you too."

I had a ritual on days like this. Days where we just enjoyed each other and the rent we paid. After we ruined the sheets, we'd take a shower, and I'd wash and detangle her hair. Then once all of that was done we'd get in bed, under a blanket fresh out the dryer, and fall asleep in each other's arms. Sated and silent.

"So hey, about tomorrow," Cleo murmured.

Unfortunately Cleo wasn't feeling the silent part tonight. We were snug under the covers, but I snapped my head around like an irritated owl at the mention of tomorrow. Initially I tried to hide my discomfort with her going off alone to meet them folks, but in the last few weeks it had grown to be a thorn in my ass. They still were yet to come check on her and they're only conversations were about what she was bringing. Safe to say I wasn't a fan.

"Did you really wait until I was fucked, fed, and in bed to bring up bad news?" I grumbled.

"Duh," she scowled. "Now you're too tired to flee."

"Ugh, fine. What's the plan for tomorrow?"

"So I figured I'd make my cornbread over here. That way yours is hot and ready."

"So far so good," I nodded.

"And that way you can load everything in the trunk for me."

"Your gas tank is on E ain't it?"

"Quarter tank," she shrugged, flashing me that infamous, mischievous grin.

I shook my head while adding the task to my mental to-do list for tomorrow. I constantly reminded her to keep her gas tank at half and she constantly ignored me. You would think she secretly enjoyed having her day interrupted by waiting on me to pull up with a gas can. Although sometimes I used it to my advantage. Especially when she didn't have her membership card...

"Where do they even live for you to think you were getting far on that?"

"Bye, Mars. I'll send you my location when I get there tomorrow."

Damn, I knew it was a 50/50 shot when I asked, but I didn't expect her to clock me immediately. So I was nosey and preferred to know her whereabouts just in case. That wasn't a crime unless it was unconsensual.

"You can't fault a nigga for trying," I shrugged.

"Sure I can. I know you love me, but Mars baby. You can't slay all my dragons."

I could if she let me.

"Sometimes I have to go through things on my own. If I get burned, lesson learned."

I disagreed. If anybody burned Cleo, I'd scorch them. I'm talking barbecue hotdog char.

"Ok, sweetheart?"

No. Absolutely not.

"I guess," I pouted.

Cleo was being a big girl about everything while I was mentally throwing a fucking fit.

I did not trust those folks.

Was that wrong of me? Yes, yes it was. But did I give a damn though? No, not really. She was mine. We both knew that. Which meant she was mine to love, mine to fuss over, and mine to protect.

This protection guarantee was rated E for everyone, even grandmas, and especially absentee ones.

"Would you stop worrying yourself about something that hasn't even happened yet and focus on holding me?" Cleo snapped.

Although I was deep in the throes of doubt, I instantly abandoned my anxious thoughts at her request.

"I'm sorry," I conceded. "Come here."

Thick curls blinded me as a soft woman nuzzled my bare chest, forcing me to finally relax. Cleo traced my arm while I messaged her back and eventually our breaths slowed as we began to fall into a well deserved slumber.

"Everything's going to be fine," Cleo grumbled.

A large part of me was still skeptical, but I repeated the mantra anyway.

"Everything's going to be fine," I parroted before falling asleep.

The Kat's Outta The Bag

Cleo

I wondered if Mars knew he was in love with a liar, because everything was not fine.

"Luci, I fucking threw up on the highway!" I screeched.

Anxiety was something I always struggled with, and it's ultimately what pushed me out of being a teacher. It had gotten better since I moved and met Mars because he had been coping with PTSD for years. He had plenty of tips and tricks on how not to lose your shit and he shared them happily. We even meditated that morning in anticipation of some unforeseen force disturbing my calm. I didn't appreciate the subtle cynicism in his suggestion but I can admit it was helpful. However as soon as I realized he wasn't sitting besides me, singing along to Get To Know Ya, my anxiety manifested all over my shirt.

I couldn't call Mars because that would've been the end of my little solo adventure once he found out I made myself sick, and despite my forty year therapist Papa assuring me that we weren't co-dependent, I had my doubts. I'd been the face of Ms. Independent my entire adult life, and suddenly I couldn't even meet my family without a man by my side?

What the fuck was that?

"First off," Luci sighed. "Are you safe?"

"Yeah, I took the first exit I could. I'm sitting in a strip mall parking lot."

"Ok good. Second off, are you possibly pregnant?"

"Hell naw. Mars is snipped and goes back for annual retesting. He has had zero swimmers since '19."

"Alright, alright. So you're anxious. What's going on?"

Suddenly I fell quiet, because I realized Mars was right to be concerned. My grandma was my one contact and she was inconsistent. We'd only spoken over the phone once, and despite me living only 20 minutes away, she'd always been too busy to meet me. I knew the bond would take time, but the warmth I hoped to feel towards the woman who birthed my dad wasn't there either. It was jarring.

"I have my doubts about all of this," I admitted. "I feel like they might reject me."

"Clo," Luci groaned. "Why are you even putting yourself through this? Just go home and use today for self care."

"No, I can't do that. Because then Mars is gonna say fuck today and cook the steaks he has marinating, then we're gonna hole up and watch movies, and he won't say I told you so, but we'll definitely both know that I proved him right without even trying. I can't inflate his ego even more."

I could hear my best friend pinch her nose through the phone. Normally I might feel bad for being so stressful, but we did it to each other. Just a few weeks ago I thought she'd get arrested for stalking her now girlfriend.

"Cleopatricia, that is such brat behavior."

"I learned it from the best. How's Maia doing by the way?"

"Don't start. We're talking about you right now. So you don't wanna tell Mars. What are you gonna do?"

"I'm gonna go in this gas station, see if they have a shirt I can fit, clean myself up, and meet my folks."

"And if it goes bad?"

"And if it goes bad, I'll save face, hop on the highway, and go cry to Mars."

"Solid plan. Let me know what time y'all wanna hop on FaceTime for a double movie date sitch."

"Bye, Luci. Love you."

"Love you more. Please let me know when you get where you're going."

Of course the only acceptable 3x shirt that EzStop had left was a cropped sweatshirt with a suggestive, Ready To Get Stuffed graphic. It was bad, but the men's 5xl with a crudely drawn naked "tiny dancer" was objectively worse. Especially since my mascara had run in the middle of me sobbing. While the hot, puke-induced sweat had my freshly straightened hair reverting back to curls. In any other case I might've taken all of these things as a sign to go back home and be honest, but I knew my weak-willed courage would buckle as soon as I stepped a toe over that threshold. So I took a deep breath, stuffed my titties back in their holder after my gas station hoe bath, and got my ass back on the road.

Mars

"Chewy! Are you coming in?"

"Yeah, give me a minute. I'm just checking on something real quick!"

I pulled into the backyard of my family's home fifteen minutes ago but I hadn't moved a muscle.

Something was wrong.

Cleo left an hour before me and she told me she was only gonna be thirty minutes away, and she still hadn't texted me anything. I had half a mind to leave and try to find her, but even I knew that was unreasonable. My sister's dogs were circling my car like sharks because the entire back seat smelled like smoked ribs. I had three racks and a pan of baked beans in my trunk. I couldn't just drive around with all of that.

Nor could I sit outside like a frustrated phantom forever.

"I swear to God, you better text me back, Cleo," I sighed as I shirked my seatbelt.

I relaxed a little once I walked through the front door. The house was decorated in deep browns and rustic oranges just like daddy preferred when he was alive, and Kara must've lit his favorite candle because it smelled like vanilla apple cider in addition to slow cooked turkey and stuffing. It was comforting, and I almost mentioned it, but then the devil spoke my name.

"About time you came in the house," Kat huffed. "I've been waiting on these ribs all day."

"Hello to you too, Katherine," I scowled as I handed off my contributions. "My drive was fine. Thanks for asking."

"Oh please, Chewy. You know what I meant. You do not have to be so damn formal all the time."

You know how folks lie and say they don't have a favorite child/sibling/cousin?

Yeah I didn't do that.

Katherine was my least favorite family member, period. She was rude, inconsiderate, and patronizing. The fact that we were siblings only made it worse. She felt like she could give me dust and I had to accept it. Which is why I only came around during the holidays.

"Chewy, how's my favorite baby brother?" Kara grinned as she fixed me a plate.

"Half brother," Kat belted out oh-so-conscendingly.

She constantly reminded people that we weren't "full blood." As if being born to a dysfunctional, elitist, borderline alcoholic mother made her better than me. It wasn't my fault that our dad fucked her best friend and made me, but she sure pretended like it was. That wrinkle worm ass bitch better hope she made good with her kids before it got too late. Because if it was left up to me she was going in a home. The shittiest one I could find too. One that offered pepper or salt. Not both.

"Stop looking so mean, Chewy," Karla cooed while patting my arm. "You know that girl ain't got no sense."

"Y'all have got to stop making excuses for her," I grumbled as I bit into a piece of turkey. "She's 74 years old."

"Ooh you so serious. How on Earth do you keep a woman?"

By not being an asshole. That was the first step. Step two was to always be in the mood to eat it like an ice cream cone.

"Chewy ain't dating nobody," Karla interjected.

"Yes, he is. What's her name again? Clover?"

"Cleo," I sighed.

"She's so sweet," Janae giggled. "I like Cleopatricia."

"Now why does that name sound so familiar?" Kat asked while pouring a whiskey.

"I said the same thing," Nae shrugged.

"I'm going to the bathroom, be right back," I hollered.

The second floor bathroom was my favorite room in the entire three story house.

Mostly because it was the quietest.

Sure the paint was peeling off the walls in some spots, and the window was drafty, but all it really needed was a fresh coat and a plant in the corner. If Kat wasn't a permanent fixture in this mother fucker, I would've done it myself months ago. Unfortunately I couldn't stand to be around her for more than five minutes at a time.

Dad would undoubtedly be disappointed with how our relationship shook out after all these years, but I tried. I tried to be patient, to hold space for her emotions, to let the slights roll off my back.

Yet it was never enough.

Kat wanted me to pay for the sins of my parents. My existence was proof of their betrayal against her and she hated me for it. Everyone could tell but no one would check her because she was a master manipulator. She'd just deny everything and insist that we were overthinking her "jokes." People like Kat were the reason I was so wary about Cleo meeting her own family. Call it projection or experience, either way I had reason for my concerns.

I was about to text Cleo and explain all of that, but my phone pinged with a long awaited message as soon as I slipped it out my pants. She was there.

I checked the pin she dropped so I could save it just in case, when I noticed it was hovering right over my current location. That couldn't be right. Were we somehow logged into the house account or something? Or maybe she was visiting some of our neighbors. I knew Mr. Clarence and Ms.Tia had kids around her dad's age. I was about to go out back and look for her car, but then I heard the doorbell ring and the screendoor to the sunporch swing open.

"Welcome! Come on in," Kat exclaimed.

Suffocating doom washed over me in waves. Who the fuck was Kat inviting in? A vampire? Everybody was already here as far as I knew. Kara and Karla's boys were out back, Janae was in the house, her sister was around here somewhere. Who else was there?

I practically galloped down the back steps to find out. I could hear a mirage of voices kee-keeing in the living room, and I couldn't distinguish a single one of them besides Kat's. I got even more pissed off when I tripped on the loose runner sticking out of the mudroom, but as soon as I turned the corner, that anger turned to fear. There she was. Thick curls, thick waist, chubby cheeks, and brown eyes that contained far away planets when the sun struck them.

The love of my life.

"Cleo? What are you doing here?" I gasped. "I thought you had a family thing."

"Mars? I a- I mean I do. What are you doing here?"

"Oh, you met Chewy?" Kat laughed. "Apologies. He's mean as hell but he sure can cook a rib."

"Katherine, shut up," I growled as I realized the situation unfolding around me.

My stomach lurched, and then my skin dotted with cool sweat. There was no way in hell.

"Cleo, are you sure this is where you supposed to be?"

"Yes, Mars. Kat is my grandma. Why are you being so antsy? What is going on?"

"No, she's not," I laughed. "Katherine is not your grandma. She only has one granddaughter named Patty."

"Yeah, short for Cleopatricia," Kat scowled. "That's a mother-fucking mouthful otherwise. And Chew-"

"Actually, I prefer Cleo."

"Ok, sure Patty. Chewy, who pissed in your cheerios? Why are you being so damn nosey all of a sudden. You never gave a damn about Janae or Antwon popping up."

"That's because they're not my-"

I threw my hands over my mouth, pushing down the urge to scream. This had to be some sort of cruel joke, a real gotcha moment.

"Mhhm. This cannot be real life

I wasn't sure if Cleo had connected the dots yet, but Katherine sure as hell hadn't.

"What cannot be real life?" Kat squawked.

Unfortunately Karla had...

"Oh my God. This fool done fucked his damn niece," she gasped.

The air around us went still. The urge to scream and maybe even break something grew. I knew life had the capacity to be cruel, but even this was too much. There was no way I avoided meaningful connections with women after all this time just to fall in love with my blood relative, and not even a distant cousin or something, but my fucking niece.

"No," Cleo turned to me in a hushed whisper with tears welling in her eyes. "Mars, tell me she's joking."

"She's not. I'm their brother."

"So your dad is my great-grandfather?"

"That sounds about right."

"Ok," she nodded with a barely withheld sob. "I need to leave."

"Cleo no, please wait," I begged.

"Nuhuh."

I tried to run after her, but Kat stopped me with a hand to my chest. "Are you really dumb enough to the point where you ain't know who she was, or are you just as nasty as your mama?"

Of course she brought up my Mama. Kat knew how to cut me. In any other situation I would've gone off like a bomb, but not now. My immediate concern was Cleo getting on the highway while she was in clear emotional distress. I knew how she got when she was upset.

"Katherine, please move," I said gently. "I need to take her home."

"Why, so you can fuck her one last time before you officially go back to being her uncle?"

"Move, Kat."

"I don't even know why I'm surprised. Look at who had y'all. She so confused, got two damn daddies, and your Mama was a gold-digging hoe."

My shoulders tightened from the increasing mental load. I just found out that the woman I planned to marry was my niece. My day had gone from bad to worse in a matter of minutes, and my oldest sister was berating me in front of the neighbors, the dog, and maybe even God, all while my anxiety was rising about Cleo getting on that highway.

"Stop it, Kat," Kara chided.

"No, because that's just nasty. That girl fucked her damn uncle and got the nerve to run out of here crying and carrying on. I hope her car-"

I had almost thirty-five years of practice taking shit from Kat so it never bothered me when she treated me like tissue paper stuck to her shoe, however Cleo was my recently acquired soft spot. Something in my brain broke when I heard her talk about *my* woman like that, and suddenly Kat being my sister wasn't a good enough reason to hold my temper.

"SHUT THE FUCK UP YOU LONELY, HATEFUL, BITCH!" I roared as I pushed past her.

I didn't bother to check for Kat's reaction as I ran out the house, but I was seconds too late, because all that was left of Cleo were the trails her tires left behind and the faint scent of her emergency car perfume. I probably wouldn't be able to catch her but I still wanted to make sure she was ok. So after going back to retrieve a pan of ribs and the bottle of wine she brought, I hopped in my car and headed south on 96. Family scandal or not, Cleo was still mine to look after.

Cleo

The first thing I did when I got home was close all the curtains and blinds. It was only three in the afternoon but the skies were unusually clear for late November and I really wasn't in the mood to see any of that cheery ass shit. The second thing I did was scream.

It was a blood-curdling scream reminiscent of 80s horror movies where the special effects were the real tragedy. The leasing office was probably going to call me about that on Monday but I needed it. I also needed a hot shower and a spiritual bath, but a bitch had to prioritize. After my scream, I picked myself up off the middle of the living room floor, put on a pot of water for comfort Mac and cheese, and dragged my ass to the shower. If I had been at Mars', I could've soaked my day away in his tub and let him wash the lingering vomit smell out of my hair.

But that was now inappropriate seeing as he was my uncle and all.

My fucking *uncle*. I don't know how we both missed the signs, but I guess we just chalked some things up to cultural coincidence. A patriarch named William? Common Black experience. Men in your family who have babies late in life? Common Black experience. Shady ass family who tried to act like their shit didn't stink? Common Black experience.

Common *Katherine* experience.

Sure, shrugging off the similarities made sense. But how didn't our names spark any concern?

Oh, duh.

Because they call that man Chewy and me Patty. Plus he had his mama's last name. Fucking black people and nicknames. Why the hell is Mars nicknamed Chewy anyway? What was the story behind that? I had half a mind to text him and ask, but my doorbell started buzzing as soon as I rinsed off the soap. And despite my attempts to ignore it, it kept ringing.

Shit.

I wasn't in the mood for guests. I was barely in the mood for the human experience as a whole. If I had more time to think about the implications of falling in love with a blood relative, I probably would've driven into the ravine on the way home. Yet I didn't, so I slipped into a robe and shuffled to the door in my house shoes, hoping to get rid of whoever it was.

Since they wouldn't take the damn hint.

I swung open the door with all my available force, and as usual, the door hit the wall before shaking like a leaf.

Unfortunately, the usual suspect was also the person darkening my door. Standing tall in his dark red plaid shirt, coordinating beanie, and thrifted corduroys. The ones with a heart shaped patch on the right thigh.

"Mars, what are you doing here?"

"I came to check on you. Also, I noticed you didn't eat. So I brought you ribs and potato salad."

I gasped because he wasn't just talking about a cute little sampling plate. He was talking about the whole hog.

"Mars Evans, did you swipe Kat's entire bowl of potato salad?"

"Yeah. I can't stand Kat, but I got to give her credit where it's due. She can throw down on some potato salad."

"Mhm."

"And occasionally cornbread. But I prefer yours now."

"I don't know if you're allowed to say that to me anymore."

"Come on, Cleo. I didn't say I wanted to eat your macaroni."

"I mean do you? I'm cooking some right now."

"That feels like a trick question, but can I come in anyway? I need to take a stress shit."

"Sure, you can blow up the bathroom."

"Hey, what's up with the nickname Chewy?" I asked between bites.

We had been eating in silence for the last thirty minutes, but I was finally slowing down enough to taste the food. The ribs, turkey legs, and macaroni were especially hitting. Sure it was petty for Mars to renege an entire pan of meat along with a pound of potato salad, but I was grateful. I hadn't realized how ravenous my appetite was until it took me 10 minutes to grate enough cheese for sauce because I kept nibbling on the block. I guess having several mental breakdowns takes a lot out of you.

"So you know how I don't like Now & Laters?" Mars sighed.

"Yeah, because they're chew- Oh my God. Are you for real!? That's how you got your nickname?"

"Basically," Mars nodded while wiping his mouth. "My Mama gave me one when I was like six and I spit it out onto the dog because I didn't like how it felt in my mouth. And when I got yelled at for it I cried, saying,

"It's too chewy!" So for a while I was Too Chewy, and eventually it just got shortened to Chewy."

I was shocked, but not really surprised. The whole house oozed mean girl energy, and really it just came from one person.

"Let me guess, Katherine?"

"You know it. That woman is... A piece of work."

"Yeah I can see that now. She gives religious psychosis vibes. Did she call me a slewfooted whore when I left? That's apparently what she used to call my mama."

"Cleo," Mars sighed.

"What? I'm just asking. She didn't even bother to tell anybody my full name when she introduced me. I bet it made the transition seamless. Now I'm probably Patty the Uncle Fucker."

I was hurting myself more than anybody ever could, and the screwed up thing was I couldn't even stop it.

I was spiraling.

Bad.

Mars did the right thing by checking on me, but all it did was make reality come back for seconds. How could he be so fucking considerate even when he knew we couldn't be together? How could he be so kind and thoughtful? It wasn't fucking fair.

It wasn't fair and there was nothing I could do about it but cry and yell. So yes, the neighbors had every right to complain, and I wouldn't so much as blink when the leasing office wrote me their passive aggressive ass note on Monday, and if Mars left I'd understand that too. But because life wasn't fair, he didn't. Instead he did his best to calm me.

"Cleopatricia, cut it out. You're making yourself sick."

"I can't, Mars. This is so fucked up, and the worst part about it is, it's all my fault. If I hadn't been so adamant about trying to reconcile a doomed relationship with Kat, we'd been in bed right now eating sweet potato pie and watching 'Who Made The Potato Salad?' I ruined everything because I didn't know how to listen."

"You didn't ruin anything, Cleo," he said soothingly as he pulled me into a hug. "Isn't it better that we know anyway?"

"No, because it doesn't erase the fact that I love you, Mars! It doesn't change the fact that I can only fall asleep if the covers smell like you. It doesn't make my heart race any less when you hit me with that goofy ass smile, or when you say my name. It only means that I can't, at least not in good conscience, have you."

I whispered that last part into his chest, hoping it wasn't loud enough for him to hear it. Hoping that we didn't have to acknowledge it so soon, or move out of this hug, or give up this feeling.

And when the only sounds to fill the room came from the pouring rain outside my living room window, I thought I had succeeded.

"I know," Mars sniffled back. "I was just hoping that you would agree anyway so it'd make this next part easier on both of us."

"Please no," I begged.

"I have to. Because if I don't do it now I'll never be able to do it. I love you, but I can't let you be demonized for this. You are my solstice and my equinox, my rise and my descent. If I could put my soul in a pendant for you to carry around, I would. You deserve the whole wide world and everything in it. I'm so sorry I couldn't be the one to give it to you, Cleo."

I couldn't find the breath to reply, so I just squeezed him tight until he had to let go, and when he kissed me before finally walking out of that raggedy ass door, I couldn't find the strength to get up off the floor either.

It's Our Anniversary

Mars- 2months later

"Don't," Jay warned.

"Don't what?"

"Nigga, don't play dumb. That's what. You cannot text your ex on the one year anniversary that you didn't make it to."

"Psh, I wasn't going to."

Actually, that is exactly what I was about to do. A year ago I asked Cleo for exclusivity after our second date and she said yes. I thought I'd be spending every February since making her smile, but instead I was doomed to an empty house and another fucking ice storm. The winter months had always been hard for me, but it was especially heinous this year. Mostly because I was still hopelessly in love with a woman who was my biological niece. That wouldn't have been a problem two-hundred-or-so years ago, but now there were laws against that.

Which was kind of bogus the longer I thought about it because we didn't really fall into either of the two situations those laws were written to prevent.

We did not want to breed offspring, and I did not groom her. We had the unfortunate pleasure of meeting as clueless adults, and while I enjoyed shooting the club up, my nuts were 100% lactose free.

"She's your blood relative, Mars."

"I know that! Could you please stop reminding me?"

It was bad enough that I could still remember what she tasted like most days. I didn't need Jay refreshing me on the fact that I loved the taste of home in more ways than one.

"No, because you look like you're about to do something reckless."

"I'm not doing anything tonight but going home and contemplating a paint thinner smoothie for the third time this week."

"Th- The third time?"

"Look, man. It's been a rough year."

Honestly the year had been wonderful up until Thanksgiving. I always resented Kat for blaming everything that had gone wrong in her 50s on me, but now I was returning the favor. She was such an abysmal mother that she had an estranged granddaughter who didn't even know who she was related to us. She was such a terrible mother that her bullshit transcended time, space, and generations. That in itself spoke volumes to her character and I reminded her every chance I got.

Hell, I'd probably inscribe that on her tombstone.

"You look like you're plotting, so all I can say as your unofficial lawyer is please don't do anything illegal. Even if strangling your sister is a long time coming, it'll still be unfavorable in court."

"Gotcha. I won't kill Katherine."

"Or Maim her..."

"Can you please just take your win and go? I'd like to sulk in peace since I'm off today."

"Fine, but I will not be bailing you out if you get locked up after 8pm. I got a hot date tonight."

"Oh, is it that time of year again? Where are you and Ronda meeting up this time?"

"Goodbye, Martian!" Jay shouted, as he exited the cafe. "Make good choices."

I probably wouldn't, but it was sweet of him to try anyway.

Made it!

I'm sorry.

My thumb glided against my phone's fingerprint sensor for the third time in twenty minutes. Unlocking and then locking as soon as I pulled up our messages. I was trying. I was trying so hard. But I could never bring myself to delete all of our pictures together, especially not the innocent ones. So of course Apple decided to remind me of how fucking ecstatic my goofy ass was this time last year, and of course that sent me on a spiral.

Being in a romantic relationship with my niece was wrong.
Duh, I knew that.
But that didn't mean we couldn't be friends. I'd take Cleo however I could get her. (Pause.) Even if she just wanted me to be the family member she occasionally sent weird food TikToks to. I just needed something, because everyday that she was out of my life felt like a needle in my already wounded heart. Everybody thought I'd be over it in a month, and honestly, I did too.
Unfortunately it just wasn't that easy.

So yes I was going to text my ex/niece/love of my life about a box of clothes that she probably didn't give a fuck about in hopes that it sparked some sort of conversation, and if she spat in my face with disgust then so be it. At least I tried.

Made it!

I'm sorry.

Hey, I found some of your stuff in the wash. Your plaid skirt and a few sweaters. Want me to bring it by when you have time?

Damn I've been looking for that skirt everywhere. I'm home now if you feel like it.

Praise Jesus! Or perhaps Lucifer? My guardian angel had to be laid up somewhere either drunk or dead, but hey that was none of my concern. I had a thirty minute drive until I was back dancing with the devil. Heaven could wait.

Should you show up to your ex's house with flowers if you had no intentions of getting back with them?

Probably not.

That was definitely toxic gaslighting shit. However, I grew these flowers specifically for Cleo. Sweet Nymph Amaryllis bulbs cost a fortune since they can't be grown from seeds, and the flowers die regardless of if they get cut or not. I had already done the work to bring them this far, so somebody might as well get to enjoy them.

And by someone, I meant Cleo. Because I'd cut anyone else over these.

I knocked twice then stepped back for when she inevitably threw the door into the adjacent wall. It happened just like that only seconds later and although it pissed Cleo off every single time, I couldn't help but smile. As shitty as life could be, some things were just guaranteed happiness.

H-hi," she gulped, with a rehearsed tone.

"Hi."

Cleo looked just as beautiful as ever. Her hair was tucked away in braids, yet it still remained wild and askew. Her cherubesque face was still radiant. Likely a great source of envy for angels and demons alike. And not that I was trying to look, but her ass was still fat.

"What's this?" she asked of the bouquet.

Her question released me from my tortured thoughts in record time. "Amaryllis that I grew. Figured you could enjoy them for the week."

The air of coolness initially surrounding Cleo dissipated as she gingerly slipped the flowers from my hand. Her pupils exploded as if she'd been dosed with something potent, and then they narrowed to stop the flow of her potential tears.

"Mars, you didn't have to," she cooed.

"I know, but I wanted to," I sighed. "You deserve beautiful things in your life no matter what."

"Shit, I swore I wouldn't cry. Damn it, Mars," she fussed while stomping her feet.

"I'm sorry."

"No, it's fine. They're just so pretty and I'm PMSing."

Right, it was that time of the month. I could almost smell the pheromones in the air. I could also smell roasted garlic though, so maybe I was having a stroke.

"Would you like to come in? I'm cooking a roast."

"Oh, are you sure? I wouldn't wanna impose."

"It's five pounds of meat, Mars. You're not imposing," she frowned. My mouth water at the prospect of a gravy laden piece of roast. God, I missed Cleo's cooking. However, everything about this felt like a bad idea. It had been two months and this felt normal, it felt comfortable. It felt like something Jay would warn me against.

But I was weak-willed when it came to Cleo, so of course I said,

Cleo

"Yes."

Dinner turned into a movie marathon, and how Mars was up getting a blanket from the hall closet because I refused to turn the heat back on. One day it was 78° and then the next 54°. I didn't know whether to bust out the fans or order more flannel sheets. The weather was flip-flopping too much for my liking, and I refused to pay Texas power anymore then I already had.

"Luci must've visited. I see you're missing blankets," Mars chuckled.

"Yeah, she stopped by for two weeks in December. The blankets were payment for her detangling my depression mat."

Luci's abilities creeped me the fuck out most days, but I couldn't have asked for a more supportive friend. I told her all about what happened with Thanksgiving and she hopped on the first plane out of Atlanta to help me pick up the pieces.

No judgement. No Lectures.

Just love and impartial advice.

"Fair trade. Hey, how many points do I have?"

"Twenty four. I got forty."

"Damn, I gotta catch up."

We were halfway through the second MIB, and spread out in front of us was a stack of index cards with the series' correlating conspiracy theories. We'd talk about them after each movie, then research them to see if they had any merit, and if they did, the writer of said theory got a point. Five points got you $1 to spend on SnackPass. So far I had enough points to buy a brownie with caramel sauce. Mars had enough for a bag of Doritos.

"Ready?" I asked, dragging my thumb over the play button.

"One sec. Let me get a bottle of water."

"Oh, can you pour me another glass of that Merlot?"

"Yeah, I want one too."

If the implication wasn't literally incestuous, I would almost say that this felt like a date. But maybe that's just because we regularly did stuff like this when we were dating. We were comfortable with each other because we weren't just in a relationship to fuck, but we were also friends. I missed my friend. I'd been trying to ignore how disjointed I felt for the last two months and failing at it because Mars was my person. Even without the spine-realigning sex. Luci warned me that I wouldn't be able to just ax him and forget. I hated proving her right.

"You alright?" he asked while eyeing me with a healthy dose of skepticism.

I accepted my wine glass and took a hearty gulp to calm my nerves before lying to the man who, at times, knew me better than I knew myself.

"I'm fine. Just thinking."

"Don't do that too much. There's a reason they say ignorance is bliss." The irony of that phrase was not lost on me at all. I was the happiest I'd ever been back when I was blissfully unaware that I was regularly sucking off my great uncle.

"Sit down. I'm ready to win this so I can eat my brownie."

"Sure, Jan. Press play."

Mars

Fuck.

I was over-confident because I did originally come here with noble intentions. But spending extended time alone with Cleo was in fact a terrible idea. Because the wine we finished off three hours ago had us drawing the curtains 40 minutes before the last movie credits rolled, and now Cleo was laying directly on top of me, dead asleep. Muscle memory was something crazy. She used to do this all the time when we spent the night, especially when it was cold. I found being her body pillow comforting once upon a time. Now it was terrifying because we would be in a very questionable position if I so much as sneezed. I felt a little shame about being rock hard underneath Cleo, but my body held the reins here. It wouldn't have been so bad if her hard nipples weren't poking me through her thin ass house dress.

Unfortunately they were though, and the longer I stayed like this, the more awkward my very necessary exit would become.

"Bab- I mean, Cleo. You're sleeping on me. You got to get up," I whined.

"Hmm," she hummed before snuggling in closer.

Thank God she never wanted to be a mother, because she slept like a brick. It didn't matter what was happening around her, once she was asleep, she was asleep. One time I moved the entire living room around while she was napping. It was impressive, but I was also terrified to leave her alone through tornado season next year. All it would take was one ill-timed nap and she'd be swept away.

"Cleopatricia!" I yelled.

She jolted up like the undead. Allowing me a perfect, unobscured view of her full breasts spilling over the top of her gown just before her ass landed squarely in my lap.

"You're sitting on my dick and I can see your nipples," I squeaked as I tried to keep my penis under control.

For a second, I was almost scared that it would cut through my clothes to get to her. Technically dicks weren't sentient, but sometimes I had my doubts.

"Oh shit, Mars. I'm sorry," she offered while rushing off of me. "What time is it?"

"I have no idea."

"Where's my phone?"

"I don't know," I grimaced as her hands brushed the top of my thighs in her search. "But that's still my dick."

"Why the fuck do you have so much dick?"

"Hey! You weren't complaining before."

"Yeah because it was mine then. Now it's my uncle's. You can't just go around telling people how heavy your uncle's dick is. That's terrible party conversation."

"God, your jokes are just... So corny," I cackled while shaking my head. "Shutup!" Cleo chuckled.

She pushed against my shoulder to show me she meant business, but it just made me laugh harder until we were holding onto each other as we wheezed in a steadying breath.

We fell back into a comfortable silence afterward, one of our usual ones where we just stared at each other. First it was eyes, and then when the eye contact became too intense, we moved on to catalog other features. I let my gaze rove over her gentle wide nose, round cheeks, and adorned ears, while Cleo focused on my chin, the grays dusting my hairline, and the scar on my upper lip. Somehow I got comfortable while focusing on the mole adorning her chin and I found myself stroking the mark with the pad of my thumb. I was disassociating. Only focusing on the warmth and softness of her skin, and then the way she felt beneath me. I paid special attention to the heat of her breath for just a second too long and before I knew it, our lips were brushing as we settled into a hungry kiss.

"Mmmm."

I didn't hesitate to broadcast my pleasure with a guttural groan. Sure, part of me knew it was wrong, but Cleo was back in my lap, and all her heat and softness pressing up against me was distracting. Her hands were exploring all of my uncovered skin while she set an eager pace with her rolling hips. I was only a man. So I gave her what she wanted. I spread my legs wider, pressed my length against the damp print of her pussy, gripped her hips with my greedy hands, and stole the breath out of her lungs. I kept kissing her until she was left breathless and confused with red, swollen lips, her needy little nipples poking holes through the thin gray cotton of her night gown, and a clit that was probably thumping. I knew fully who she was to me, and I didn't care. All I wanted was to spread her open, take my fill, and make her sing my name the same way she did every evening two months ago.

And I knew she would let me.

Cleo

"I'll stop if you want me to," Mars rasped as he traced my outer nipple.

This was a slippery slope in more ways than one, and I probably should've told him to stop, but we both knew I wouldn't. We were both out of control and the only thing separating our bodies from our future sins were two pieces of cotton and the looming knowledge that we were more to each other than just our love and sex.

Unfortunately I didn't really care about that.

I just wanted him to put his mouth on me.

So I slipped both breasts out of my flimsy ass gown and watched silently as he flicked his tongue against my right nipple and then my left before ultimately attempting to suck them both in tandem. The soothing glide of his skilled tongue against my tight areola had me unraveling within seconds. I even let a quiet moan escape me when Mars slipped his hand between my legs. His touch was gentle but thorough as he worked my pulsing clit underneath his thumb. Poor Pearl. She'd gone so long without the good shit that she was leaking all over the place after just one touch. I watched with a strange mix of awe and pride as I leaked down his thick, veiny wrist and made a mess of the couch cushion. His coaxing touch inspired me, and soon I was pulling down the waist band of his sweats with my teeth.

"Fuck, Cleo," Mars hissed as my nose touched his pelvis. "Why would you do that, pretty girl?"

I simply giggled as I relished the feeling of my mouth stretching around him. It felt so nice to finally slobber on it again. I took my time with him. Bobbing, licking and sucking until his chocolate dick looked like it was covered in bubble solution, rubbing the seam of his ballsack between my thumb and middle finger, and occasionally teasing his tight asshole with a quick sweep. Mars seemed to appreciate that the least, but he never once asked me to stop. Instead he was trying to politely refrain from fucking my face as if I was new to this. I had to manually push his hips to get him to catch on and finally choke me like I wanted.

Of course it took him no time at all to release all of his hesitation down my throat. Mars came with a lip pinched tight between his canines as he cursed me. Then once he was done calling on God and Satan alike, he pushed me on my back to return the favor. I don't even think it had stopped twitching before he had his mouth on my clit, slurping down all my stress and frustration as I rubbed his lil shiny head like a magic 8 ball.

"Damn it, Mars," I moaned. "Why are you so fucking good at this?"

"Because I like to study," he teased before returning to his business.

Mars was born to eat pussy.

He could slurp down an entire bowl of spaghetti straight up, no hands. Which is why I wasn't very surprised when he wrestled a nut from me in record time. I also wasn't surprised when I felt his warm drool drip into my ass afterwards.

He always cleaned his full plate.

I survived twenty minutes of torture before he was satisfied, and when my last belly-shaking orgasm was finished, he flipped me onto my stomach and pressed my body into the carpet with his. I was aware of every muscle, callous, and scar as he settled against me, and I wanted all of it. Yet when I arched my back, inviting something more, Mars raised his hips to avoid it.

"Is that all you want from me, Cleo?" he asked with a slight hiss. "Did you just want me to lick your pretty pussy and spit in your ass? I won't be mad if you say yes."

I understood he was trying to give me room to change my mind, but I hadn't. Despite knowing the truth I still wanted him fully and wholly without reservations.

"Please," I whimpered while squeezing my legs together.

Mars was patient, but he was also rubbing his tip against my slit in slow circles, getting it all nice and wet for when he finally heard what he wanted to hear. I could practically feel him coming inside and stretching me out every time he lingered at my entrance. I was beyond ready.

"Mars, please."

"Please what, Cleo? Do you want me to leave?"

"No, Mars. Please fuck me."

"Are you sure, Mamas? I'll probably make a really big mess and make you sleep in it. So then you'll smell like me in the morning."

"Fuck. Me," I gritted.

I arched my back again expecting him to comply since my consent was so clear, but instead he sat onto his haunches and spread my ass cheeks.

"What are you doing?" I fussed before his actions silenced me.

It took Mars all of five seconds to fill me completely with that marvelously wide dick of his. My pussy spasmed as I settled into the sensation of being stretched out and stuffed, while Mars sat behind me watching every twitch and pucker with a deviant grin.

"I just wanted a reminder of what you looked like wrapped around my dick," he growled before pushing my body back down.

Our speed increased once I adjusted, and soon I had the same question as earlier.

Why the fuck did he have so much dick?

It was cruel for a man to be blessed with both a big dick and a capable tongue. Not for him, but for his lover. How was I ever supposed to get over the soft way he kissed me and the liquid motion of his hips? This was supposed to be wrong, but as our flesh collided in the middle of my living room rug, all I could think about was how perfect it felt when we were together.

"Cleo, I missed my pussy so much," Mars moaned while nipping my ear. "Shit I missed you, Mamas. Look at how well you take me.

Look at how wet you get for me. You like this shit, baby? Do I make you feel good?"

"Soooo good," I cried while dragging my nails against the carpet. "So fucking good."

I felt connected with the heavens, the earth, the grass, and hell, even the crickets, as Mars did his best to become one with me.

"Is this pussy mine?" he asked as he palmed my ass.

"Yes."

"Cleo, I asked you if this pussy was mine?"

"It is," I whined.

"Then tell me it's mine, baby. Tell me it's mine."

"It's yours, Mars. Fuck your pussy-"

I almost went with the classic, "daddy", but instead I decided to take the unique opportunity given to me and cry about it later.

"Fuck your pussy, Big Unc," I giggled.

Mars let out the most appalled gasp I ever heard, but he didn't dare stop stroking me. Instead he draped himself
over my back to drill me deeper as his head shook from side to side.

"I guess I deserved that for calling your jokes corny all the time, but you gone pay for that, baby," he groaned.

Two months wasn't a long time to be apart in most cases, but it was long enough to make me forget just how vindictive Mars could be. I thought he was just gonna dig me out until I was one with the floor, but apparently he intended to make the next super villain.

One of his arms came behind my left leg and pushed my knee into my elbow while the other bracketed me against him.

Deep wasn't the word.

His strokes were now exhaustive. His hips were playing arco, rising and falling with such precision that they summoned a song from the briskest depths of hell. I cried out in sorrow with Mars as we fell victim to an accelerated pace.

One. Two. Three.

One.

Two.

Three. Four.

A half a minute later I couldn't even keep count. I just knew that this was the beginning of the end.

"Ooh Cleo, I love you," Mars panted as he held me tighter. "I love you so much, Mamas. I'm sorry that I'm doing this to you."

"It's ok," I wheezed. "I want it."

I deserved it actually. All the unhurried pleasure, all the lust-drunk kisses, and all the counter-clockwise strokes that ended in me convulsing like the possessed while the man I loved wore my pussy out.

I deserved every good thing that happened tonight, but I especially earned those last few lazy strokes that allowed me to feel Mars' cum drip out of me. He looked so proud after he saw the mess we made together. So I think I missed that the most.

"Can I hold you for a little while?" he asked as he slipped out.

Actually I lied. Lying on his chest and listening to his steady heart beat until I fell asleep was my favorite thing in the whole world. That was what I missed the most.

Who in divine orchestration decided to make this man my damn uncle? I needed them to come outside. I just wanted to talk.

Mars

Cats had the right idea when it came to cuddling. Kneading people was relaxing, especially when they were plump, and Cleo was so chubby. I massaged her soft valleys until we were both boneless and sleepy, but she decided to ruin all my hard work once I tucked my nose into the crook of her neck.

"Maybe we don't have to give this up completely. Maybe we can just be sneaky links."

"Cleo, what?" I asked with judgement dripping from my voice.

"No, you're right. I'm sorry," she offered. "I don't know why I said that. I just. I missed you and I want you in my life even if it's secretly."

I sat up in a frustrated huff. Was that really what she thought of me? That I was just some depraved ass nigga who wanted to fuck his niece in secret?

Well jokes on her because I wasn't.

I was much worse than that.

"Cleo, I can't fuck you in secret. I'm in love with you. I wasn't joking when I said that. I don't wanna be your occasional dick, I wanna be your man."

"Oh."

"Yeah, oh."

"Ok but serious question. Outside of Kat and what she'd have to say, why can't we be together? It's not like we want to have kids. You didn't diddle me as a child."

"Please don't phrase it like that."

"I'm just saying. What's the big deal if we're not passing down our bad joints to some poor unfortunate soul?"

"Honestly, Cleo. I don't know. I've been asking Jay that for weeks now. All he keeps telling me is that there are more unrelated fish in the sea."

"What if we moved away and didn't tell anyone?"

"Cleopatricia."

"Mars?"

"Ok, but where would we even live?" I asked as if this was actually a feasible plan.

I don't know why I was entertaining her on this. For one, two-thirty in the morning was no time to have life-altering conversations. Then for two, I couldn't just pull a Hades, kidnap my niece, and move to another part of the world.

Could I?

"Washington is nice," she shrugged.

"You would rather keel over than regularly spend $500 on braids. Plus it rains a lot there. Very overcast. You need regular sunshine. You're already prone to vitamin D deficiency as it is."

"Mm. You're right. What about Maryland?"

"Baltimore or DC?"

"Baltimore."

"That could work. It's far. But what about your parents? What about Luci?"

"Luci knew I was never gonna get over you. She'll visit, I'm sure. We can figure it out with my parents. What about Jay though?"

"He actually recommended that I block you months ago," I said, sweeping her braids from her eyes.

"Ouch. Although I get it. Because now we're about to run away together."

"Are we? Maybe I'm not convinced."

"You are," she grinned as she curled her nails into my beard.

She didn't know that for sure. Baltimore was nice, true. The food was good. It was close to the coast. I wouldn't have much of a problem finding a job out there, not that I ever did. Plus there would be plenty of opportunities for Cleo.

"I don't know, baby. I'd be incinerating any sliver of chance you had to be close to your dad's side."

Yeah I didn't give a fuck months ago, but that's when I thought they were perfect strangers. While I personally couldn't say she'd be missing much with Kat, I couldn't assume that Cleo felt the same. Things changed.

"I've seen all I need to see," Cleo said gently. "It doesn't really matter now anyway. There will always be rumors about us. They're gonna retell that story every Thanksgiving. We might as well make the ostracization worthwhile."

She had a good point. Many good points actually. I heard a new remix of what happened almost daily. Karla's sons were claiming that at some point Cleo sucked me off in the downstairs bathroom for her own pan of ribs. Would I really miss them folks? Probably not. Still...

"Why is this making sense? What am I missing?"

"It makes sense because we're in love, Mars. Unfortunately we can't just take it back. And to be honest, I wouldn't want to anyway. Meeting you revived my joy of the human experience. I knew you were gonna be my person."

"I wanted to marry you," I admitted with a tearful mumble. "I actually still have the ring. I couldn't convince myself to get rid of it."

The tears slid down my cheeks once a vision of our would-be proposal populated in my mind. I hated crying. It had been like that since I was a kid. I didn't like what it did to my senses, and I especially didn't appreciate the vulnerability it induced. However now I could say that I was thankful for that part. Because Cleo dried my tears with her palms and held me close until my breathing evened out. Until I was ready to be honest.

"We can't take this rug," I mumbled.

"Why because it's too big?"

"No, because it needs to be professionally cleaned and maybe exorcized. Getting it back to normal would probably cost a small fortune, and I do not want to explain how this happened."

"Fair enough. You'll buy me a new one."

"Yeah, I will."

I know her neighbors would be grateful when she moved, because it sounded like a comedy show in here any time we were together. Laughter bounced off the walls and the ceiling for two minutes straight until we ran out of breath.

"Mars?" she sighed.

"Yes, Cleo?"

"I'm still really thankful for meeting you even though I'm about to ruin your life."

"I'm so thankful for meeting you, baby. You make my days infinitely brighter. So don't worry about it, we can build a new one."

"So is that a yes?"

"It's a yes, baby. Happy one year anniversary."

The End.

Thank You!

Hey Friendddd! So obviously, you finished the book, and I just wanted to take a moment to say thank you. You may want to cuss at me after this, and that's valid, but just know that Black representation in romance is important to me, and that does include taboo romance. I can't say that I'll do this again but I can say that it was a nice challenge. I recently passed my two year publishing anniversary and wow, what a way we have come. From conquering big wide knowledge gaps, to building ARC teams, and even my first signing event, y'all have held me down. Thank you so so much for all the love and support. I really could not ask for a better literary community, and as always, I look forward to catching you at the next book!

P.S.

If you liked this book, please consider leaving me a review. It helps others in the community discover my work!

Kat's Favorite Ribs

Mars' one saving grace? He could make a fire ass rib. Best served alongside a slice of white bread, a scoop of macaroni, and a heaping of potato salad. Stolen or otherwise. Serves 4-6 people.

Ok, boom. The recipe:

Optional (not really) brine:

- 1/2 cup salt

- 3 tbsp brown sugar

- 2 tbsp black pepper

- 1/4 apple cider vinegar

- 1 whole orange with washed peel

- 4 cloves of garlic

Water to cover your meat completely. Let brine for at least 4-8 hours or overnight preferably.

The rub:

- One pound of pork or beef baby back ribs

- 1/4 cup of apple butter+ 2tbsps set aside.

- 1/4 cup Dijon mustard

- 1/4 cup garlic powder

- 1/4 cup onion powder

- 1 tbsp salt

- 2 tsp black pepper

- 2 tbsp paprika

- 1 tsp chili powder

- 2tsp allspice powder

- 1/2 tsp cumin

- 1/2 cup of preferred ale (set aside)

Prepare your ribs by rinsing them and then removing the silver membrane along the back. Place ribs in a large dish or tupperware container alongside your salt, sugar, pepper, garlic, oranges, and vinegar, and then fill the container with warm water until the meat is covered completely. Brine for at least 4-8 hours but no longer than twelve. After brining, preheat your oven or grill to 350° F, discard all of your solution except for ¼cup, pat your ribs dry with clean paper towels, and arrange on a tray. Mix together apple butter and mustard, adding in your additional seasonings until a paste is formed. Massage the paste into the ribs, then place the foil wrapped ribs in the oven or grill meat side up for 45 minutes. Once thirty minutes have passed, mix your reserved brine, ale, and apple butter, then apply the solution to your ribs every fifteen minutes for 2 hours or until your ribs have reached an internal temperature of 200° F. Once desired doneness is reached, remove ribs from the grill or oven allow to cool, and then serve alongside your favorite sides. Enjoy!

Also by Aria

Glory
https://www.amazon.com/dp/B0D1YH9BNH

Burry The Hatchette
https://www.amazon.com/dp/B0CT34SSS4

Candy Corn Curses
https://www.amazon.com/dp/B0DJLQ3W14

Rudy Jones's New Year's Resolution
https://www.amazon.com/dp/B0CLMWNPQJ

From Kingston, With Love
https://www.amazon.com/dp/B0CPDFXY9P

Bloom
https://www.amazon.com/dp/B0C82QWN2F

Candid
https://www.amazon.com/dp/B0BZMZVZ47

Human Resources

https://www.amazon.com/dp/B0DMR5NY9X

About the author

A ria is a die-hard romantic and her main goal is to always be drying her eyes from something sickly sweet. She has been dreaming up romance stories since she was seven years old, with the first one being a Toy Story fanfic. She's also a Neo-soul and R&B enthusiast who's forever got a song stuck in her head. You can find her looking for good food, reading, writing, or enjoying time with her family in her free time. She lives happily in Saint Louis, Missouri with her middle school sweetheart-turned-husband and their adorably chaotic son. Her dream is to one day write inclusive stories that center BIPOC full-time, but for now, she labors in fraud as a working stay-at-home mom.